smash
into you

SHELLY CRANE

Cover design by Okay Creations
Photo, Photo Shoot, and Promo Photos by K Keeton Designs
Cover models: Taylor Grass and Elizabeth Underwood
Interior Design by Angela McLaurin, Fictional Formats

ISBN-13:978-1491234518
ISBN-10: 1491234512

Printed in the USA

1 2 3 4 5 6 7 8 9 10

More information can be found at the author's website:
http://shellycrane.blogspot.com

"No longer a boy who lost it all, I was a man that realized how much I had to lose."

    - Jude

- M. Leighton, NYT Bestselling Author of Madly and Down To You

"Caleb is the sweet, sexy, smart guy every girl dreams about--me included!"
- Nichole Chase, NYT Bestselling Author of Suddenly Royal

"Caleb's sweet, fierce about Maggie, valiant, honorable, gentle, noble."
- BookNerdsAcrossAmerica Book Blog

"There were gorgeous scenes in which Caleb left me breathless."
- Misty Provencher, Author of Hale Maree and Cornerstone

"Shelly Crane is full of talent and this book just became my favorite of all time. I can't even begin to explain what this book did for/to me."
- Lindsay Paige, Author of the Bold As Love series and Panic

For my two boys
May you always know how to treat a girl, how to respect her, how to love her for who she is, focus on the things you love about each other and compromise everything else, make it work, make it last, adore her. She's yours. Protect, love, and cherish her.

ONE

It was a case of mistaken identity.

The kind that ended with appalled, parted lips and evil glares.

The worst kind.

The girl was cute. Adorable really. Cute and adorable wasn't the problem or the solution for me. I needed to blend and be invisible in the most plain-as-day way and girls like this, girls who just walked up to guys because they had hope somewhere deep inside them that I would fall for that pretty face, were the opposite of plain-as-day. Those kinds of girls got guys killed. At least the kind of guy that was on the run.

She had mistaken me for a normal guy.

And this girl who approached, who could see that I was already surrounded by one already, which was one more than I needed, must've thought I had a hankering for something sweet. Because when she spoke, her words were soft and almost made me want to get to know her instead of sending her packing. But I couldn't stay in this town. It was better to hurt her now when she wasn't invested than it would be to leave one day without a trace.

The girl who was currently soaking up my attention—that she thought she had—she'd move on to her next prey and forget I ever existed. But sweet girls like this got attached and asked questions.

Don't stop running...

My eyes met hers and a buzz went through my body. The strange sadness in her eyes matched something in mine, meaning that she hadn't had an easy life either. Gah...this girl wasn't just beautiful, she was adorable and sweet and sad all wrapped up in a package that would be so easy to accept. It was way more appealing than the current materialistic succubus in pink attached to my arm right then. I swallowed and stared as bored as I could at the girl as she finally made her way to me from across the hall.

She tucked her hair behind her ear gently and smiled a little. "Hi, uh, can I just-"

Showtime. "Honey, that's real sweet, but I'm not interested." I slid my arm around my groupie. I didn't even know her name, but they were always within arm's reach. "As you can see, I have my hands full already, but thanks for offering."

She scoffed and looked completely shocked. I took her in, head to foot. She *was* really adorable. She had a great little body on her and her face was almond shaped. Her lips looked…sweet. She was not the kind I wanted within ten feet of me. She was still standing there. I had to send her packing…to save her in the long run.

I grinned as evilly as I could muster and felt a small twinge of guilt at the vulnerable look of her. I looked away quickly. I didn't even want to remember her face. "Run along, darlin'. Go find a tuba player. I'm sure he's more your speed. Like I said, I'm not interested."

She didn't glare, and that was a first. Most of the girls who approached a guy were confident. I mean that was the reason they thought they had a chance, right? But she looked a little…destroyed. When her lips parted, it was in shock—it was to catch her breath. I continued my bored stance, though at this point, it pained me in my chest.

But I was doing the best thing for this and any other girl. People who got involved with me were collateral damage when Biloxi came around. He was a ruthless bastard and if he found me and knew someone cared about me, or worse, that I cared about someone, he'd be all over them.

So when she turned without a word and swiftly made her way down the hall, I was thankful.

I probably saved her life, though she had no idea. She thought I was an ass, but I was really looking out for her. That's what I told myself as I watched her go. That I had hurt her feelings for a reason, and that she'd get over it in no time.

A slender hand crawled over my collar.

"What's this from?" she asked in a purr and slid her thumb over the long scar from my ear all the way to my chin. She hadn't even acknowledged the girl at all and now, didn't give a flip either. It hadn't even crossed her mind that I might be more interested in that other girl. "Mmm, it's so sexy."

It followed my jaw line and it was absolutely not sexy. Unfortunately, it wasn't the first time some girl had said as much and it pissed me off to no end that they thought that, let alone said it out loud.

It was my reminder of what happened when I let my guard down and it was anything but sexy.

I bit down on my retort and sent her a small smile that showed her I was listening, but she had to work for it. "Is that right?"

"Mmhmm," she said and kissed my jaw. "I have a little scar, too." She pointed to the place between her breasts. "Right here. Wanna see it?"

I managed a chuckle. "Is there really a scar there?"

One of her friends, who was also on my arm from time to time, joined her, looping her arm through hers.

"Pick me up tonight and you can find out," the succubus purred, making her friend giggle.

"Don't think so, darlin'. Busy."

"Ahhh, boo." She pouted and let her other hand hook a finger into my waistband. "Well here's something to keep you company tonight."

She pulled me down by my collar and kissed me. I tried not to cringe away, but her lipgloss was sticky and sweet. When she tried to open my mouth with her tongue, I pushed her away gently with my hands wrapped around her bony arms.

"Let's keep this PG, honey. Settle down."

She giggled. I knew she would.

It was the last week of school. It was my last week to pretend that I was still *in* high school. The next time I made a move to evade Biloxi, I'd enroll in college because I was getting too old to be a high schooler. I didn't know where I was going. I would have graduated from high school already, but at the rate I was going, I didn't know if I would have *actually* graduated or not. School was not a place of learning for me, it was a cover, a place to blend in and be normal until Biloxi found me and then I'd be gone to the next place.

This was my life. No time or want for long-term girls, no fun, no movies, no parents.

This was my life, but it wasn't a life at all.

Two years, eight months, and three lonely birthdays later…

College towns sucked.

The big one.

I had only been here for a few weeks. It was part of my cover. I practically chanted those words in my mind as I trudged everywhere I went and worked my butt off. But one thing remained the same. Desperate girls ran rampant and I still wasn't interested. Every once in a while, they were good for a distraction if need be, but mostly…not interested. Not really, not anymore. My eighteen-year-old self ate up the fact that girls seemed to want me, with no strings attached, but after months of that and a long list of girls I never saw again, it got old real fast.

And then sometimes they said no strings attached, but didn't mean it. There was this one chick, Kate, who would not take no for an answer. She'd 'found' me over the summer when I was apartment hunting and hadn't 'lost' me yet, no matter how hard I tried. To get her to go away one time, I'd even given her my phone number. I was going to ditch it in a few weeks anyway when I undoubtedly had to move again, so it didn't matter, right?

Wrong.

The girl was as annoying as a Chihuahua all hopped up 'cause there's a knock at the door. The texting and come-hithers were nonstop.

Life wasn't turning out as fun as it had been back when I was eighteen.

And now, as I stared out into the dark rain to see a POS car sideways in the road, I knew the world hated me, had to, because someone had just smashed their car into my truck.

I got out and braced myself. It wasn't easy to pay cash for new cars every time I needed to skip town. It was hard living when you couldn't be who you really were. Finding work and people to pay you under the table was almost impossible these days.

I groaned and glared at the beauty standing at the end of my truck. "Look at that!"

"I'm so sorry," she began. I could tell she really was, but I was beyond pissed. "I'll call my insurance company right now."

That stopped me. "No!" I shouted and she jolted at the verbal assault. "No insurance."

"Well," she pondered, "what do you mean? I have good insurance."

"But I don't."

She turned her head a bit in thought and then her mouth fell open as she realized what I was saying. "You don't have *any* insurance, do you?"

"No," I answered. "Look. Whatever, we'll just call this even-steven, because you did hit *me*."

"Even-steven my butt!" she yelled and scurried to jump in front of me, blocking my way.

"And what a cute butt it is."

Even through the noise of water hitting metal, I heard her intake of breath. The rain pelted us in the dark. I hoped no one came around the corner. It would be hard for them to see us here in the middle of the road. She might get hurt. Then I wondered why I cared.

"Look, buddy," she replied and crossed her arms. It drew my eyes to her shirt. My eyes bulged 'cause that shirt...well, it was see-through now. She caught on and jerked her crossed arms higher. "How dare you! You're on a roll in the jerkface department, you know that!"

"My specialty," I said, saluting as I climbed in my truck. "Get your pretty butt in your car and let's pretend this never happened, shall we?"

Because if cops and insurance were brought into this, I'd be on the run sooner than I thought.

She huffed. "Excuse me-"

"Darling. Car. Now." She glared. "Like right now."

She threw her hands up in the air and yelled, "I knew chivalry was dead!" before climbing in her car and driving away. She didn't know it, but I was being as chivalrous as they came. I made sure she got out of the rain and back into her car, even though she didn't like the way I did it, and I got her as far away from me as I could.

In my book, I deserved a freaking medal for being so chivalrous. Because people that stuck with me didn't live long.

Just ask my mom.

Oh, wait, you can't. She died a long, long time ago saving my life. I refused to bring anyone onto this sinking ship with me. If it finally did go down, I was going down alone.

I made my way back to my place and parked in the lot. I took the stairs two at a time to my crappy apartment and plopped myself on my bed, feeling a sudden exhaustion settle over me...the facade, the lies, the daily life of me, wore down on me like rubber sneakers on pavement. I felt raw and ground up. I wondered how long I could actually live like this before I collapsed in on myself.

The tune of *Bohemian Rhapsody* alerted me that I had a message. I jerked it from my front pocket and looked at the text from Zander. He was the school's resident party boy and he was definitely the kind of guy that I always found when I went to a new town. Because a guy that threw parties on the fly could *get things*, and for a guy on the run, I needed someone like that. In fact the fake ID I was currently sporting with a different last name was from him. I texted him back that, yeah, I'd come to the anti-frat party he was throwing tomorrow night. I had no classes. I only took one elective night class, which was only in session two nights a week, just so I could say that I was a college student there, but I really wasn't. And the class? Freaking Spanish.

Odio españoles.

I showed up to work with exactly thirty-seven seconds to spare. I blamed gorgeous-smash-into-me-girl. I swore my truck was acting funny and I had no cash to fix it.

I nodded to Pepe, the owner, and winked at Mesha, the wife of the owner. She giggled behind her hand, and so our day began just like every other day. Pepe owned a feed store and the guy had muscles the size of tangerines. So, that was my job description. In fact, on occasion, he even called me that instead of-

"Hey, we need muscle up here!"

I shook my head. "Yep!"

I trotted up front to help the dude in duds load thirteen bags of chicken feed. It wasn't a glamorous job by any means, and the pay was *caca*, but it kept me fit and busy. That was what I needed. If I had to up and leave, I wouldn't be leaving the guy in a jam because guys like me were a dime a dozen.

The day wore on and at punch-out time, I felt a familiar hand reach across my back. Slither was more like it. "Hey, Jude."

"Mesha," I mumbled back without turning and rolled my annoyed eyes. Were all women the same? They never wanted me for anything but a good time and then *see ya later*. Which was great for my life, but dang did it get old. Especially since the tune never changed.

"Pepe's playing cards tonight." The insinuation hissed from her lips in what I'm sure she thought was a sexy whisper. It made my skin crawl.

"That's great for him." I grabbed my metal lunchbox and turned the other way, the long way around the back, but it was worth it to evade her.

"That's it?" she practically yelled. "I thought you'd jump on it?"

I stopped. Dang. She just caught me on a wrong day. I turned. "Why? Because of what you've got between your legs? Darlin', there are a hundred girls on speed dial. Sorry. I'm a busy guy."

And wait for it..."You're such an ass, Jude! I was just testing you anyway!"

I waved above my head and kept going. Women. Typical.

I threw my lunchbox through the open truck window and prayed it would start as I climbed in. She sputtered, but held out, I'll give her that. I tapped and rubbed the dash. "Come on, girl. Come on."

She cranked and I drove straight to the auto parts place. I popped the hood and waved away the heated smoke. Sighing, I closed my eyes. Mother...this was going to cost a paycheck to fix, which I didn't have to spare. I went inside and priced a radiator. I almost punched the man in his teeth when he told me the price. "Are they made with titanium now and I'm just out of the loop?"

"Economy's bad for everyone, son."

I held the counter with both hands and hung my head. "Well...dang."

"Look, uh, I might need a little help here tomorrow. If you come help me for the day, I'll take half off the radiator, all right?"

I looked up, unable to stop the incredulous look. People didn't do good deeds for nothing. It just wasn't the world we lived in any longer. But I looked up into the older man's eyes and saw that he was serious. There was a story there. A son, maybe, a nephew, he was trying to make up for. I didn't want to know. I didn't want to get attached.

"You serious?"

"Dead," he countered.

I spoke slowly, "OK. I can be here at around two when I get off from my job. That all right?"

"Yep. I need some help stocking the shelves, so that's perfect. I'll work you a full eight hours," he warned.

"It's worth it." I swallowed and hesitated. "Thank you."

"Sure thing, son."

I nodded and turned to head back to my busted truck, not real sure what to think. But for now, I'd take it.

As soon as I got home—barely because the truck overheated again—I showered and threw on some clean jeans with my boots and a button-up. The party was going strong by the time I arrived. Zander met me in a flourish at the door, the nonstop host. He offered me smokes and dopes and every kind of liquor under the sun. I waved him off and took a soda from the fridge. I never had been much of a drinker, and taking things to make me disoriented and off my game wasn't smart for someone who needed his head on straight at all times. I hopped up on the counter and nodded my head to some of the guys that always hung around Zander. "Hey, man."

"Jude! Didn't think you'd make it," one of them yelled over the music and bumped my fist. "Dude, the honeys are in full force tonight." He grinned this calculated little grin. "Zetas are here, dude. Zetas."

I laughed. "I thought this was an anti-frat party?"

"Fraternity, no. Sorority, yes!"

I shook my head as he took off laughing. "Idiot," I muttered under my breath with a laugh.

"Who, me?" I heard the sugary voice and dreaded looking up. I didn't even know why I came out. I didn't think I had the energy to play this game tonight.

I lifted my face to find one of the party circle regulars. She wasn't one of those awful girls who slept with anything that hit on her and purred all over you. She was a harmless flirt and a pretty sweet girl. Which was why I always tried to steer clear. Sweet and harmless meant I'd just hurt them instead. I couldn't do it. "Hey, Lila. How's it going?"

She sipped her red Solo cup and shook her head in a cute, noncommittal way. "Ehh. There are way too many girls here tonight." She peeked back and laughed at Zander trying to keep up with someone on the dance floor. "See? How can I compete with *that*?"

We both watched as the clearly intoxicated girl fell all over the place in her gyrations. "Yeah," I agreed. "All right. See you later."

"Wanna dance later, maybe?" I hated the hopefulness in her voice.

"Nah, not tonight." I hopped down and left without a backwards glance, calling over my shoulder. "See you around, OK?"

They were playing Eminem and I was so over it. This whole scene...just over it. Maybe it was time to start looking for a new identity. Instead of college towns, maybe I could try a farm town or something. I was young, but had been forced to grow up too much, too fast, too soon. I just wanted quiet and peace, even if for just a small amount of time.

On my way out, I waved to Zander so he would know I was gone. Just as I turned back, lightning struck up my spine. Daggum....it was her.

The girl who crashed into me.

My feet made up their mind before my head did and I was walking her way. She was leaning against the hall wall by the stairs and was currently being cornered by a guy with two red cups in his hands. She was politely trying to wave him off while simultaneously looking for someone in the crowd. Or maybe that was just a decoy move to make this guy go away.

Before I could think, I found myself helping her with that problem. "Beat it."

He looked over his shoulder and scoffed. "I'm sorry. Do I know you?"

"You're going to know me very well if you don't scram. It doesn't look like she wants to talk." I looked at her face for the first time and knew she knew exactly who I was...given by the heinous glare I was currently receiving. I crossed my arms and cocked my head a little. "Do you want to talk to him, darlin'?"

She opened her mouth to rebut, but must have thought better of it. She stared at my face and seemed to have another revelation. The shape of her lips changed as she looked back at two-cups-McGee and she smiled a little at him. "Thanks for the offer, but my boyfriend finally made it. He'll get me something to drink."

She moved out from behind him and stood beside me, but not close enough to touch. I found myself twinging with regret about that and frowned. There was something about this girl that was twisting me inside out.

"OK," the guy drawled and lifted one of his cups in a farewell wave. "Sorry, man. Didn't know she was with you."

She scoffed as she watched him go. "Of course he apologizes to *you*."

I ignored her sneer and decided to start digging my own grave. "Is your boyfriend really here?"

"Don't have one. Don't want one." She looked me right in the eyes. "Don't need one."

The words didn't matter. The only thing that existed in that second were those lips. The night we 'met', it was dark and raining, and though it was obvious then how gorgeous she was, it was also obvious now that she was different. She had a little scar on her top right lip that she probably hated as much as I hated my scar, but God help me...I wanted to kiss that scar a million times over right then. Her hair was blond and hung in loose curls around her shoulders. She was wearing cowboy boots with her jean shorts, and her shirt was definitely not see-through tonight, but she was wearing long sleeves though it was hotter than piss outside. Her eyes wandered in an uncomfortable way as she looked around the room at anything but me. She had a couple scars on her neck that looked like chicken pocks or something. She tugged at her sleeves and looked at the floor as if gathering courage.

This wasn't a normal girl.

Dang...and she was trouble.

"Well...I'll see you." I turned to go and was surprised when her little hand shot out to stop me. Her hand couldn't wrap around my arm and her eyes bulged a little before she dropped her hand and looked at me again. Her eyes were blue. Dang...

"You send that guy away and now you're just going to give me the ol' *See ya later?* What the hell? Maybe I wanted that guy to give me a drink."

"If that's true, then why did you look so relieved and say I was your boyfriend?"

"That doesn't matter. First, you hit me with your big, stupid truck-"

"You hit me," I corrected with a grin.

"-and then come in here, all Neanderthal like, and make the males scatter before hitting the road? What gives?"

I kept my grin in place. "I don't like to see a lady take a cup full of the date rape drug. That's all."

"You're right. I'm eighty-nine percent sure it was full of the date rape drug, which is why I would have never taken it. But thanks anyway." She shuffled her boots. Good Lord, it was adorable. "So you can be chivalrous here—why not be chivalrous at a car accident?"

My grin fell. What the hell was I doing? She was right. I had no business being here. I cleared my throat. "Like I said, I'll be going. Have a good night..." I hadn't meant to pause for her name. I didn't want to know. It would just make things worse-

"Marley," she snapped. "The girl you crashed into and threw in her car to let her deal with her own car troubles name is Marley."

"Nice to meet you, Marley. I'll see you around."

She scoffed as I turned. "He really doesn't remember. Or care."

I didn't stick around to find out what she meant.

THREE

I woke before my alarm clock went off. I couldn't stop thinking about that girl. Marley. She didn't eat up my every word, she called me on my crap instead. She was just...something I'd never encountered before. I couldn't put my finger on it, but it was evident that I needed to stay away from her. I had a big, long, busy day ahead of me and could think of no better way than that to keep my mind occupied.

That day, as I hauled bags of feed and used my arms until the muscles burned, I found myself hoping her car was all right. That afternoon, I made my way over to the parts store. I hopped out of the truck, swinging the door open before jerking to a stop as a car sped from the lot. My gut twisted with fear, but I felt my brow crease with a frown. It couldn't have been Biloxi. He would have come after me right then and there. He wouldn't wait. That wasn't his style. I had been running from that man, and the people he worked for, every second that I could remember of my life.

I didn't know what they wanted. I didn't know who they were or where they came from. All I did know was that I had something they wanted. My mother died trying to keep me from them. It had been too long since I'd seen him. Three months was some kind of record for us.

In fact, it made me even more on edge that it had been that long, and not for lack of my trying to evade him. I was good at laying low, but as much I hated him, he was good at finding me.

Biloxi, Mississippi. That was the place where my mother was killed. Biloxi was now his name until I could find him for myself. Then I'd call him by his real name as I choked the life from his throat.

"Son?"

I looked inside to find the old store owner looking at me expectantly. "Yes, sir. Coming."

He led the way to the back room and showed me the piles and piles of boxes to be stacked. The man was really going to make me work for it. I nodded to him and got to it. I heard the front door bell ding several times and voices carry as he helped his customers. I tried not to be paranoid about Biloxi and just get the work done.

The bell rang again and a female voice asked sweetly for help to find the right taillight. Lightning shot up my spine again. I inched my head past the shelving to see the girl who was hell bent on destroying me. I cursed under my breath. I took a deep breath and got back to work. I'd just ignore her and she wouldn't even know I was back here.

"Jude? Can you bring me a box on shelf L3C? It's on the bottom right."

Dang. I almost just said, 'Screw it', and bolted, but I owed the guy. So I got the box he requested and shuffled, grumbling, out to the front. As soon as she saw me, the fire in her eyes sparked. I felt the sides of my lips tug.

Daggum adorable girl.

"You," she sneered in surprise.

"You," I rebutted and winked. "And how are we tonight, darlin'?"

"Well, I've got a busted taillight thanks to you. I got pulled over." She reached into her purse, searching for something. "Like I can freaking afford an eighty-five dollar ticket."

For the first time in a long time, I felt a heap of guilt settle in my chest. "Listen..." She looked up, exhaustion and frustration spelled all over her face. "I'm sorry about that. There are just some things that you don't understand about me."

I looked at the owner. He was giving me a funny look. I looked back to her and that sexy, scarred lip of hers.

"I get it," she said, surprising me, and sighed. "I can barely afford my own insurance. I work at the cafe on Edgemont Street during the day and a bar at night and barely make it. I'm sure working at a place like this, you don't make much money either." She cringed and looked at the owner. "No offense."

"None taken, miss," he said and looked at me, as if it was my turn and he was enjoying all this—thoroughly.

"It's a little more of a problem than just can't afford the insurance..." I frowned before smirking my winning grin. "I'm a dirty, rotten scoundrel. I know."

She cracked a small smile. "You're right. You are. Scoundrels leave girls in the middle of the road-"

"Uhuh. I did *not* leave you in the road." I leaned my hip on the counter, bringing me just a little bit closer to her. "I made sure you were safely in your car and on your way."

She nodded and smiled like she had a secret. "That's true. Your method could use some work, though."

I grinned. "Sorry. In my defense, it was raining and it was dark."

She scoffed and laughed. "It rains and gets dark all the time in Alabama! That's not a license to be a jerk."

"You're right. My mistake," I whispered.

She looked up and latched onto my gaze. Held it captive. My insides squirmed with the need to run, but fought for the right to stay. Lucky for her, *run* won.

"Anyway, let me pay for your taillight at least." I took out my wallet and tried for a smile. "Then we can at least part as friends."

Her smile shook. "I thought you went to school here?"

"I do...but I'm pretty busy. I doubt that we'll run into each other again."

She bit into her bottom lip. "So you won't be hitting me with your truck and then saving me from drunk guys on a regular basis?"

I chuckled. "I hope not."

Her face showed disappointment. Even after everything I did to her, she still wanted to see me? This girl was my conundrum.

"Well..." She took the box in her hand. "Thanks, I guess."

She turned to go. I watched in a strange agony, a pull over me so strong to follow her. Ask her out, take her to get a coffee. Anything. But the thought of her meeting the same fate as my mother stopped me from doing any of those things.

I turned to go and the owner grabbed my arm. "Why didn't you ask that pretty thing out? She obviously wanted you to."

I smiled, glad that he noticed, but unable to do anything about it. "That's why I had to let her go."

He laughed and slapped my back. "Son, that makes no sense."

"I know." I smiled, but didn't feel it. I didn't feel it at all.

I took the radiator, paid him what I owed him, and thanked him for letting me work off the rest of it. He said he always had odd jobs and if I was ever in a bind for some cash, come see him. I swear that man almost made me believe in humanity again. Almost. It was late when I finally made it home. My cell had a couple of texts that I ignored. When I showed up at my door, I realized I should have answered them.

"Jude," she crooned. Yes, *crooned.*

"Kate," I said, unable to mask my annoyance. "When someone doesn't answer the phone, that's not an invitation to come to their house."

smash into you

"You haven't returned my calls." She stood from the step and revealed the short, strapless sundress she wore. "I've just missed you lately. And when you didn't answer the phone, I wanted to check on you."

"I'm perfectly fine. Just busy."

I tried to go around her, but she wasn't having it. She followed close behind as I unlocked the door. I sighed. I wasn't opening this door. She'd come in and never leave. So, though I despised the idea, I turned and looked at her. I jingled the keys in my hand and made myself grin at her. "Darlin', I'm tired. Worked all day. I'm ready for sleep."

"We can sleep," she said coyly, resting her hand on my stomach. "We sleep good together, don't we?"

"Alone," I corrected, but knew I had to do something. I leaned down and closed my eyes. Without even my permission, a cute little scarred lip and blue eyes came into mind as I let my lips touch hers. She grabbed the back of my neck and pressed me to her. I knew Kate. I knew what she tasted like and I knew what she wanted. I had misjudged her in the beginning when I just wanted a distraction. She hadn't been who I thought. She was clingy, and every now and then I came across one of them. But things were just changing for me.

I felt tired. All the time. Tired of life. Tired of this scene, this same scenario.

I touched her cheek as I pulled away from her to soothe the sting of my words. "Go on home, OK? I need to sleep. Had a long day."

"OK." She gripped my shirt front and smiled small. She really was a gorgeous girl that just needed some self-respect. "But don't wait so long to call, Jude. I miss you and I can help you relax when you have a bad day."

I smiled. "Bye, Kate."

"Bye, baby," she whispered, kissing my cheek before sauntering away, obviously thinking I was enjoying the show.

I turned to my door and out of the corner of my eye found my neighbor, an old, crabby man who had no love for me, giving me the stink-eye as he looked between Kate and me. I waved and smiled. "And how are you today, Mr. Fowler?"

"Eat me," he grumbled and kept going. "And keep it down in there!"

"Alrighty then," I laughed and went inside.

The scalding shower felt like heaven in a box. My muscles quivered and stung with relief from all the work I'd done. Honestly, I was getting hard skin everywhere and my shirts were almost too tight in the arms as it was. I wasn't one of those guys that needed to be ripped, but if I didn't move on soon, or at least get another job, I was going to have to get a new wardrobe.

I got out and stood on the mat to air dry. That was the great thing about living alone. I shaved and ran my fingers through my shaggy hair. It had gotten to be a dark blond since I hadn't been in the sun in a while. The first time I hit the beach, it would lighten up a lot.

I brushed my teeth, spitting the gritty, cheap toothpaste out into the cracked sink. As I turned, I got a glimpse of the other reminder of who and what I was. On my stomach was a large, round scar. I'd always had it. My mom told me 'they' gave it to me. It was some kinda IV port or something. Though why they would need to put IVs in me, I didn't know, and apparently didn't have the mind capacity to come up with a plausible explanation. Mom never said. I was too young when she died, only seven years ago—I was fourteen. Mom and I were in Biloxi where we'd been for a few weeks. I was brushing my teeth, they busted through the back door, and Mom jumped in the bathroom with me. I was angry at her because I was in my boxers and embarrassed. I didn't know they were there. When she opened the window, I knew. I climbed out first and jumped down. She came out next and her foot caught. She didn't break her fall on her feet like I had and she groaned as her leg twisted.

I remembered that she hobbled along with me. We thought we'd made it when we reached the edge of the yard, but sirens blared in the distance right before a shot. I turned and watched as she gave me the most regretful look. Her hand gripped her stomach and I knew everything was about to change for me. She'd been shot. She slid to the ground.

I saw *him* coming across the yard. Mom looked at him and back to me with pleading eyes. "Run, baby."

"No, Mom, no." I was embarrassed again as I felt a tear drop from my nose. My knees hurt in the dry, hard, rocky gravel, but I stayed right there. Right there with her.

"You listen to me, Jude Ezra Jackson. You've got to go without me. Now."

"No!"

"Yes." She touched my cheek and the sob that held me together broke free in a wild noise because I knew this was it. This one moment would be my last with her. "Son, know that you were never my burden, you were my joy. I wanted you, I fought for you, and you were the best thing that I ever did. I love you, Jude. Hey, Jude, take a sad song and make it better...right, baby?"

I nodded and gripped her hand tighter as her own grip began to fail. She looked over as the cop car slammed to a halt in the road. Her eyes were wild and pleading. "Go, baby. I love you."

"Mom..." I just couldn't. I knew I should go, but I just couldn't leave her there.

Her eyes began to roll a little and her breath shuddered in her throat. She looked at me once more, a tear sliding the slowest I'd seen one fall down her cheek. "Never...stop...running."

Her eyes didn't close. That was the worst horror of it all. She was watching me, but her body was no longer occupied. I lifted my gaze to see a silhouette in the dark of the man who plagued us everywhere we went. The cop got out, gun drawn as he searched the area. The man took off running the opposite way, but not before looking back once more at me. As if to say, this is far from over.

I had to agree. In my mind, it was just beginning.

In only my boxers and dirty knees, I bolted through the woods. I stayed in the brush of bushes behind the buildings in the small town. When I came to a laundry mat, I stole clothes that were too big for me and then stole my first meal. I swiped three apples from the churchyard. I remember, as I pulled those apples from that tree and looked up at the stained-glass windows, thinking that I was going straight to hell with a too-big Blimpy's Subs t-shirt on.

Later, I realized that God knew how much I needed to eat that night, and how much I needed to eat every night after that, because no matter how bleak things looked, and though I did go through nights of hunger and sleeping on benches, I somehow always survived.

And as I looked at that cracked sink in my crappy apartment, I couldn't help but be thankful to still be alive. Still be capable of hunting down that bastard one day and doing to him exactly what he'd done to my mother. Still capable of revenge. I didn't know if I was capable of more than that.

Love? Compassion? Regret? Didn't know.

Revenge? Absolutely.

FOUR

"There's homemade apple pie in the break room for lunch if you want some, Jude."

I looked over at him in confusion. He shrugged. "The wife was up early baking them. She never bakes so enjoy it while you can."

I turned so he wouldn't see me when I rolled my eyes and tossed the bag of feed into the truck. "Goody. Thanks."

"Something going on with you lately?" I looked back at him. His brow was cocked in a way that made me think it was more than just inquisitive.

"What do you mean?"

"You're just acting weird, is all."

I turned back to my task. "Nah, man. I'm peachy."

"Do you have something you want to tell me, Jude?" I knew that tone. Dang... His freaking wife was trying to get me fired.

"Not a thing."

"Jude!" he bellowed. I sighed deep before turning and putting my hands on top of the truck. "Look at me!"

"What? Spit it out. You've obviously got something you want to confront me about."

He grimaced and spit on the pavement next to us. He watched the ground as he said, "I think she's cheating on me. I know it. Have you..." He met my gaze. "Have you seen anything around the shop? Somebody hanging around after I leave or something?"

Relief flooded me. I wasn't losing my job, but that wife of his was definitely cheating on him. "I wish I had, man, so you could go get that bastard, but I haven't. Sorry."

"Well," he shook his head, "just be glad you don't have a woman, Jude. They're fun for a while, you fall in love with them, and then they slowly rip your heart out."

I chuckled under my breath. "That's beautiful, man."

"It's true!" he insisted in a loud hiss. "All right, that's all for today."

"But the day's not up." I checked the busted clock on the wall. "We've still got an hour and a half."

"Go ahead. Go home. I'll pay you for the full day. I just want to get out of here and drown my sorrows."

I brushed my hands off. "If you're sure, I've got no complaints."

"Nah, go ahead." He was pitiful, kicking his feet like a kid that lost at dodgeball.

"Want some company?"

His lips curled up. "Really?"

"Yeah, sure." I clocked out and nodded my head for him. "Come on, I'll drive. I have a feeling I'll need to be the designated tonight."

"I'll just catch a cab home later," he said, hurrying to my truck.

"You're not gonna know your own name later, let alone what street you live on."

He scoffed a 'pfft', but then thought about it. "Maybe. We'll see." He grinned and beat his hand on the top of the open window to the tune of whatever was on the radio as I pulled out of the parking lot. "I never get to go out with the guys!"

I didn't know if I constituted as 'guys', but for now, I took it. I found myself laughing at him as he sang along and starting drumming on the dash wildly with his forefingers. I thought this was going to be a somber night, but instead, it was different. He was free.

He drank enough for us both to be under the table. I shook my head as I finished off my third water and watched him dance with the jukebox. The dive we were in was somewhere I'd been often. Not this particular one, but there's a million out there just like it. In every town, there's at least one and you can always find it and just be *gone* for a while in the booze and girls.

Another notion my mom would be *so* proud of.

"Are you following me?"

My spine shot straight and lightning made my breath catch. I turned slowly to find the spitfirey, gorgeous girl who had messed my daggum truck up. I felt my lips turn up in a smirk. "Well, well, well. You just can't stay away from me, can you?"

She laughed and shook her head, obviously knowing it was a line, but choosing to go with it anyway. "Oh, please. I work here, pal, and last I recall, you don't."

She worked in a place like this with drunken idiots grabbing at her? A place that I never thought I even possessed started to burn with a slow fire.

My lips fell open in surprise as my gut churned and ached with protectiveness.

She waved her hand in front of me. "Earth to Jude."

"You remember my name." It was not a question.

She tugged and pulled at the collar of her tight t-shirt. "Yeah. You don't remember mine?"

"No." I shook my head and will admit, it was a little add to my ego when she looked disappointed. "I do not remember your name, Marley."

She rolled her eyes and smiled. "Ha ha." One hand went to her hip and the other pointed at me, the rag in her fingers dangled there. "And do not make any jokes about the name. A girl named Marley in a bar, I know, but the *Marley wanna ride my Harley* jokes are hilarious," she said sarcastically.

I laughed and stood from the stool. I peeked over to check on Pepe. He and the jukebox were still making love to each other, so I focused back on sweet face. It didn't escape my notice how she took a step back to avoid being in any personal space of mine. "Well, you point me to the guy that says that tonight, and I'll make sure he sings a different tune."

"Aww, you'd maim someone for me? *How sweet*."

I felt a chuckle bubble up. "Watch it now. I might think you're flirting with me."

She frowned a little, but still managed a small smile, and twisted her collar again. "I've got to get back to work."

I watched her skin...that soft, touchable skin. If I was never going to see her again, what would it harm? I stepped closer, her chest almost touching mine, and let my thumb trace from her brow, down her nose, stopping at her lips. They parted under my thumb and I knew then my grave mistake when I was barely successful at keeping my groan at bay.

But she didn't need to know that.

I let my fingers ease onto her jaw and lowered my head to hers. I had to let myself have this if I was going to stay away from her...just once. My lips touched her ear, and she shivered and gasped in my grasp.

"Another time, another place, Marley, and this would be more than goodbye. Don't let these jerks mess with you. You're better than they will ever be." I paused, more for me than her. I didn't want to let go and that scared the ever-loving mess out of me. "Bye, sweetheart."

When I leaned back, she had that kiss-me look. It wasn't her fault. It was just the passion-filled look girls got in their eyes when their body responded to something pleasurable in a sexual way. She probably wasn't even aware of it. I needed to run. Now.

I turned to go and found Pepe in a heap by the wall. Perfect timing. I threw his arm over my neck and hefted him up. He laughed. "Jude! I missed you, buddy!"

"Oh, I'm sure you did. Say goodbye to your lover over there."

He looked at the jukebox sadly. "She sings to me all day and doesn't ask for anything but a freaking quarter. A quarter, Jude! She's a good girl. She would never cheat."

"That's only because she's chained to the wall, Pepe."

I looked back, expecting to find an empty space where we'd been, but she was still in the exact same spot. She looked like she wanted to say something as she stared right into my eyes, her blond hair framing her sweet face, her cream cowboy boots and long legs. I couldn't let her.

I hoisted him around and was just opening the door when I heard it. It sounded like an engine, but it wasn't stopping. My instinct kicked in a split second too late as a truck came smashing through the side of the building...heading straight for my sweet-faced girl.

I moved before I realized I was. Pepe was falling back against the wall, but he was OK.

Marley was about to be anything but. Her wide eyes begged me to do something, anything, as I barreled toward her. It was all playing out before my eyes like slow motion. I didn't know if I was going to make it. Was I going to have to watch as she was run down?

My feet pushed harder and I reached her, wrapping my arms around her waist and pulling her to my chest. I hated how she felt like a rag doll getting thrown around as we swung around and twisted to the floor. I managed to take the brunt of the collision and grunted as something stabbed and sliced into my right shoulder.

There was no time to worry about that.

I stared up at the truck as it smashed into the bar. Marley quivered and whimpered in my arms, but even that didn't drown out what I saw next.

Biloxi.

He stared at me through the passenger window and I knew we had seconds left. He moved slowly and tried to open his door, but it was jammed by the broken bar. He took the gun I knew so well out of his jacket pocket and fired once, breaking the window. Marley screamed as she realized this wasn't some accident where a jackass fell asleep on the freeway and crashed into the first object.

I rolled and jerked Marley up with me as I took off. I looked back to see him climbing over the gearshift in the old Ford to come to the other side.

I felt bad about leaving Pepe there, but he'd get a ride for sure now. Cops would be all over this place in no time. I ran with Marley's wrist in my grasp and was punched in the gut with the knowledge that she hadn't once tried to stop me. She trusted me and that was worse than anything else I'd ever felt, because that meant I could get her killed if she stayed with me. I needed to get her out of there and then ditch her on my way out of town. No other way to keep her safe than that.

I opened the passenger door and lifted her up into it. I ran around to the other side, just as I saw him emerge from the bar. "Get down!" I yelled and grabbed her head, jerking it down into the seat too roughly. I floored it and fishtailed in the dirt parking lot before I hit the pavement.

Finally, when she sat up, as expected, she said it. "What the hell is going on, Jude?"

Her voice was no longer the strong, spitfire girl I was learning, now she was so scared her voice shook. I looked at her and saw blood on the sleeve of her shirt. "No, what happened?" I bellowed and pulled her to me since I couldn't pull over. We weren't out of the woods yet if he snagged a car and followed us.

"It's not me," she said softly, looking at me strangely. My hand was wrapped around her thigh where I had grabbed her to bring her across the seat.

"What do you mean?"

"You're hurt." She gulped and exhaled, her breath skating across my cheek. Her breath smelled like peppermints from the bar. She sat up on her knees in the seat and tried to look at my shoulder. The way her chest brushed my arm had me gritting my teeth. Then the tingles started before the spike of pain. I remembered now. And now that the adrenaline was winding down, the pain was coming to the surface.

I shook off her hand. "It's fine. Don't worry about it."

She steeled her face. "You're going to let me look at this. You pulled me out of there while that guy was firing a freaking gun, you're hurt, now we're running away from something—I don't know what, but you're going to tell me—and you *will* let me look at this so I can see why there's so much blood."

Daggum. "Fine," I bit out. The least she touched me the better, but whatever. I was about to drop her off. It wasn't like she had time to help me anyway.

She moved, her knees touching my thighs as she leaned over me. She pulled the collar of my shirt over and hissed. "You must've gotten sliced by the shoe guard on the floor by the bar. Mark said their boots were tearing the bar up, so he had it installed, but I've caught my foot on it a couple times." She leaned back to see my face. "It's kinda sharp. And nasty. We need to clean this up." She looked at it again. "You might even need stitches."

"No stitches because that requires hospitals." I kept up my search for headlights in the rearview mirror. "Where do you live? I'll drop you off."

She bit into her lip, a sure sign that I wasn't going to like her answer. "I'm not going home. You need me to help-"

"You're going home," I said louder. "You can't stay with me."

"I can't go home," she sulked and gulped. She sat roughly in the seat, not scooting over so we were still touching. She whispered to herself, "Oh, great. I'm going to have to tell you, aren't I?"

"Tell me what?" I barked.

"Let's just go to the drugstore, I'll fix you up, and then you can drop me off at the police station or something. I'll get a ride from there."

"I'm not dropping you off anywhere but home at midnight. Where do you live?"

She sighed and scooted all the way over to her door. I wanted to punch myself for missing her. She looked out her window and puffed a breath. It made a fog cloud on the glass. "Marley," I prompted.

"I live in my car, OK?"

I blinked, looked at the road, and then blinked some more. "What?"

"I was a foster kid. They kicked me out of the system when I was eighteen. I got a job, but I've never been able to really...keep up. With the cost of classes and everything...I live in my car."

What the hell was I supposed to say to that? There was no way I was going to take her to go sleep in her car when Biloxi just plowed through her place of employment. Speaking of, she was probably out of a job now. Daggumit.

She scoffed. "Silence is what usually accompanies that little confession." Her laugh was humorless and the way she gripped her collar, as if she were hanging on for her life, made my stomach flip. "Just drop me off at the nearest place and I'll be fine."

"Like hell I'm just dropping you off somewhere," I heard myself say. I squeezed my eyes shut for just a second or two. "Marley..." I sighed.

"Just ditch me. So what." She scoffed yet again, like she was used to people just throwing her away. "It's not like you know me."

"I *am* going to ditch you!" I heard myself growl. I gripped the steering wheel tighter, remembering this was for her own good. "You're right. I don't know you and I've got to leave. That guy...he's after me. Has been for as long as I can remember." She whipped her gaze back to mine. "So yes, I'm ditching you. I've got to."

She shook her head. "Wow. The ol' *I'm a spy* bit?" She looked at me expectantly, as if waiting for me to say *gotcha* or something. "Really?" I just glanced at her and then back to the road. "What's next? You're an FBI agent and I can't tell anyone or you'll have to kill me?"

I just stayed silent. There was just no use in saying anything. She thought I was a jerk so let her just keep right on thinking that.

She pointed out the window to an old drugstore. "Turn in here."

"I told you I'll be fine," I argued.

"Turn. In. Here," she growled in an angry, husky voice. I looked over and felt that growl all the way to my toes. What the hell was happening to me? This girl was reducing me to mush over the stupidest things. And she was aggravating as all get out, obviously had some daddy issues that would come into play later on, needed someone to take care of her—which sure as hell wasn't going to be me—and had managed to disarm me in more ways than one after she messed up my truck. The girl was batting five for five.

Needless to say, I turned into the drugstore, parking in the back. As I turned off the ignition, I thought to myself that this could actually work to my advantage. Biloxi would expect me to skip town as soon as possible, most times without even going to my apartment to get my things. I didn't own much anyway, but still. I turned to her. She was looking at my shoulder. The worry was all over her face and though I couldn't help her in any other way, I could at least let her know that I was going to be fine. I got out quickly, wincing as the cut on my shoulder pulled, and came to her side. She had just opened her door. I took her hands and helped her down. She seemed a little taken aback by the gesture, but I just leaned in. "Are you sure you weren't hurt?"

She shook her head. "No, I'm fine." She started to walk with my hand guiding her swiftly on her back. She stopped and looked back at me. "You're not to blame, you know that right?" She didn't wait for my answer. "Whoever that guy is made the decision to do that and risk others while he searched for you. You can't feel bad that you're just trying to survive." Her eyes took on a faraway look. She said, "You do a lot of things to survive, sometimes things you're not proud of, but when someone's after you, forcing your hand? That is completely not your fault."

I didn't respond to that. What would be the point? We'd get into a debate about how I'm such a bastard, and how she thinks I'm not, but I know deep, deep in my guts that I am and deserve everything that happens to me because I was born. I burdened my mother and she died trying to save me. Nah...I wasn't about to do that.

I pushed her to the back door. It dinged at our entrance and I searched around for what we needed. And when I found it, I searched for the clerk, but I was going to have to steal it. He was in the front, stacking boxes of candy, humming as he worked. I took a pack of gauze and stacked it onto my arms, along with antiseptic and some butterfly bandages and tape. I didn't know how bad it was really, but it hurt like a mother.

I pushed Marley into the smallest bathroom known to man in the back and locked it behind us. She looked around puzzled, but before she could answer, I explained. "Just in case we need something else. Otherwise we'd blow this joint."

She nodded, moving back to lean against the sink as I started to peel off the shirt, but the pain

SHELLY CRANE

was quickly chasing my breath through my veins. It was all hitting me as I slowed down. This wasn't some little cut and I was sure I probably did need stitches like Marley had said.

"Let me do it," she said softly and began to push my ripped shirt from my shoulder. I grimaced and cursed under my breath. "Sorry," she said sincerely.

"It's fine. Just do it," I said gruffly.

She pushed it down quickly and all I was left with was my black wife-beater. She looked at the shirt and tossed it into the trash can before coming back, searching the wound with her eyes. I leaned back on the door as she opened the peroxide. She took my arm and leaned me over the sink before pouring the freezing liquid over my skin. I know they say peroxide isn't supposed to sting, but it hurt so badly I hissed through my teeth. Then the bubbles started and it felt like my skin was boiling.

"Gosh, Jude," she whispered. If I wasn't in so much pain, I would have thought it was adorable. "The more it bubbles, the more germs. I told you that shoe guard is disgusting."

"I believe you," I spouted. "Just fix it...please."

"Wow," she remarked and poured another spill of the evil liquid on my shoulder. "A please and everything."

I didn't say anything, and when she started to dab and clean the wound, I just hung onto the sink and prayed for this to be over soon. She told me to lean back on the counter. She put the butterfly bandages on, and even before she said that I did need stitches and it wasn't going to hold for very long, I already knew it. I shook my head. "It'll have to do for now."

She wrapped the bandage and tape around my shoulder, securing it all in place, making sure it was tight. She was leaning on me, her hip resting on my thigh as she reached my shoulder and back. I could hear every breath, see every hair delicately out of place that escaped her ponytail, every little freckle on her skin that was right there for my perusal as she worked on me.

She wasn't beautiful in the super obvious way like the head cheerleader or Miss America. She wasn't fake looking. Her tan was all natural, her hair was blond because God made it that way, and her hips and legs were full and luscious because she ate like a human being and wasn't afraid of meat like some girls I'd known. Then I realized that all of my assumptions could be completely off, but I didn't think so.

I wanted to find out if I was right or not. As I smelled her right here next to me, I wanted to know if she was a Barbie underneath the girl I saw before me, or if she truly was the real girl I hoped for.

She leaned back and looked into my eyes, all concerned and genuine. "Is that too tight? Is it OK?"

I was losing my freaking mind. "It's fine, Marley." A too-long pause. "Thank you."

She licked her lips. "I just know you're going to be hurting later."

"Can't worry about that now. Here." I took her sleeve in my fist and ripped it along the seam, and then moved on to the next one.

"Um...what are you doing?" she asked as she watched me rip the sleeves off her t-shirt.

"You had blood on your shirt," I explained and gave her a once over. "There. Now no one will think anything of it."

She looked at herself in the mirror. "I wouldn't have thought of that. You're pretty crafty." She looked at me in the mirror behind her. "Thanks."

"Wouldn't want someone to think I beat you or something," I said and gripped her hand, dragging her with me out of the bathroom to the back door of the store. I called out, "Thank you, sir!"

"Have a good day now!" he called back with a blind wave.

I saw Marley grab a big bottle of Ibuprofen and a couple other things right before we reached the exit. We hopped in the truck and I locked the doors.

I drove us out to a diner on the edge of town, parked in the back, and went in to wait out Biloxi. I wanted to see if he'd skip town before I did. I swiped my ball cap from behind the seat and weaved my way to the back booth by the jukebox where we couldn't be seen. I knew I was drawing attention with my arm all bandaged up, but as long as it wasn't the wrong attention, I didn't give two craps.

She held her hand out and waited. I put mine under hers and four small, brown pills dropped into it. "Take it," she ordered. Again, my insides mushed and churned. Why the hell was it such a turn on to be bossed around by this little girl?

I popped them back, lifted the glass of water to my lips, and swallowed. I even opened my mouth to show her they were gone like they make you do at hospitals. Or so I figured. I'd never been to one. Only seen it on TV.

She sat across from me and as I pretended to look at the menu, I watched her. She had just followed me in the diner, shadowing my footsteps and looking defeated. Her lips were moving, like she was biting the inside of her lip nervously. Her eyes stared at the tabletop that didn't match anything else in the place. A decorating job botched all to hell. Her fingers rolled a black pen that was left on the table back and forth. Guilt took my guts and squeezed them.

I couldn't take her with me. I just couldn't. She'd get killed and I'd have another female death on my conscience. So after a little time had passed, I would take her to her car, against my better judgment. I was picking the lesser of two evils, you could say.

I leaned down trying to catch her gaze. "I'm sorry you got dragged into this."

Her face stayed the same, but her eyes looked up at me. "Still going with that crazy story, huh?"

"It's the only story I got." I snapped open the menu again and pretended that there wasn't cheese or some other byproduct stuck to the pages. "You want something?"

She glared at me. "What? Poor little homeless girl can't buy herself a turkey sandwich?"

"I wanna eat. All I was doing was asking if you did, too. Pay for your own, I don't give a..." I sighed. "Whatever. Just consider it a farewell slash thank you gift and let me buy you dinner."

She didn't say anything. The waitress came and asked what we wanted to drink and if we were ready. I nodded, not bothering to ask about Marley.

"I'll take a sweet tea, the biggest burger you've got, and chili fries. Thanks, darlin'."

She winked. "And you, honey?" she asked Marley.

Marley just stared at the table, not even looking at the menu, and said, "A big glass of orange juice, a side of green beans, a side of fruit, and a BLT on wheat, extra tomato and extra bacon, please."

The waitress just nodded and left. I stared at the girl across from me. What the hell kinda order was that?

"What? Why do you care what I eat?"

Had I said that out loud? "Uh...just strange is all."

"I like to balance out my meals."

We stayed silent until the food came and I watched in stupefied fascination as she picked up her green beans like French fries and ate them with her fingers. Then she did the same with a piece of fruit. Then she did the same to her sandwich, picking the tomato out of the bread and devouring it, licking her fingers.

I'd never been so turned on by a slice of tomato before. I clenched my teeth and tried to look away, but then she picked up another green bean and nibbled it. Nibbled it! Even I heard my growl as I leaned back in my seat. My shoulder hit the wood behind me. I cringed and gritted my teeth. "There's a fork there," I said.

"I don't use forks."

"Got a problem with silver? Are you a child of the moon and I just wasn't aware?"

She sneered. "Ha. Freaking. Ha. No, I just...nothing."

"What? You can burden me with your secret. I'm never going to see you again anyway."

She stared at me. "You're really leaving? Like for good."

"I'm really leaving. I have to." I took a monster bite of my burger.

She swallowed and blinked. "You're so nonchalant about it. Like it doesn't even matter."

"It doesn't. I've done it so many times...I can't even count."

She nodded, pensive. "I moved a lot, too, but I was never as happy about it as you are."

"I'm not happy about it. It's just something I've always had to do."

"All by yourself?" she questioned. She nibbled that green bean...nibbled...

"Not always." I gave her a look that said everything. "And no, I don't want to talk about it."

"Hmmm..." she mumbled. "She must have been a great girl."

I stilled. My eyes found hers. I knew she was probing and I should tell her to screw off, but...I wanted to tell her. I spoke softly, hoping the bitterness in me wasn't going to scare her. "My mom did everything to keep me safe from them...even gave her life."

She stopped nibbling and stared. Her eyes began to fill just a little. Just enough to make me see that it was absolutely genuine and she was heartbroken for me.

"I'm...so sorry." She shook her head and looked at the table, running her finger over a name carved into the wood. "I know that's lame when people say that, but I don't know what else to say." I started to speak, but she glanced up and my pulse banged in my ears at the look she was giving me. "I get it now. I get why you're so jaded and just push people, you don't let anyone in because you're afraid that by getting attached to you, they'll be dragged down with you."

Daggum perceptive girl... "So you believe me now, about being on the run?"

"It doesn't really matter, Jude. You're on the run in your heart and nothing I say or do can change that."

I almost scoffed. Almost.

"Eat your beans, Marley." I smiled slowly and shook my head. "We need to get going."

She smiled, too. A little shy smile that said she didn't know why I was smiling, but she just couldn't help but answer it. She ate her entire plate, every bit, and never touched her fork. Those green beans were my nemesis and as I watched her, and yes, I watched, she was completely oblivious.

When we were done, I paid and Marley didn't put up a fight like I thought she would. I wondered how much after tuition would she even have left over. I couldn't imagine it would be much. The one class I took cost a small fortune on its own.

I checked around and then towed her to the truck swiftly. I hoisted her inside and ran to my side. My arm was throbbing, even after taking the pills. I was trying to hide it because if I told her how much it hurt, she wouldn't leave and I was unable to make her.

I drove carefully, my hat pulled low over my forehead. The key wasn't to keep turning your head in looking, that was suspicious, it was to face forward and let your eyes wander. When we made it back to the bar, I was a little worried. My white knuckles ached from their steering wheel grip as we passed the tree line and saw the demolished bar. Marley gasped and glued herself to her window to get the best look. I shook my head. Biloxi cared for no one or nothing. I was going to find out one day what he wanted from me. What was so daggum important that he'd risk killing people for it? For me?

And then I saw him. The cops and fireman walked around under the whirring lights of all colors, but it was the man digging through Marley's car that had my attention.

Biloxi.

"Hell," I spouted in an angry whisper.

"What? Wha-" She saw him and stopped. "Why are they looking through my car?" She looked at me and she believed now. "Is that the guy?"

"Yes."

"But why..."

"Because I took you with me?" I wondered aloud. "God, Marley..." What had I done? It was too late to save her. "I'm so sorry. I thought I was keeping you safe by taking you with me, but I was wrong. Now he thinks he can get to me through you. He knows who you are now."

"It's not like I have an address he can find me at, Jude."

"What address did you give the bar when you applied?"

She looked sheepish and tucked her hair behind her ear. "This little abandoned house on Oxford. But it's all locked up. I've never slept there or anything."

Biloxi slammed the door to her car in anger and then jumped in the front. In no time, he had it hotwired, unbeknownst to the cops who were preoccupied, and was spinning in the gravel heading out the back entrance.

It clicked. I had an idea where the bastard was going and so, I followed him slowly. When we came to Oxford Street, I slowed even more. Biloxi was there, out of the car already, and I waited for him to go knock and interrogate Marley, because he figured either she was there or we were hiding there.

Instead, he pulled his gun that I knew all too well from inside his jacket, the silencer on the end making it protrude, and opened fire on Marley's supposed house.

I stared in shock. He wasn't even going to interrogate her to find me? He was just going to kill her? But...why wouldn't he try to lure me back with her, or hold her hostage to make me come back? My truck wasn't there...he knew I wasn't there with her... He knew that we left together...

Something wasn't adding up. What the hell did he want with Marley?

The trembling on my side registered too late. I looked over at her. She was pressed to my side, her eyes wide as she watched this man demolish her supposed home. It wasn't the home that was upsetting, it was the fact that he obviously thought she was inside it.

The sob seemed to be stuck in her throat and her breaths were ragged. Her fingers were wrapped in my shirt and she was hanging on for life.

See, this was what I was talking about. I didn't know how to take care of somebody. I wasn't capable of doing and being all the things a girl like her needed me to. But I pulled my arm around her, ignoring the sting and ache from moving the wound. She melted into my side and got as close as she could get, but she couldn't look away. I pulled her face over with my other hand, keeping my arm firmly around her. She looked wild and unhinged.

"Hide right here," I told her gently and pulled her face to my neck. "You don't need to see that."

With her face pressed into my skin, I slowly edged us down the street, Biloxi none the wiser.

Damn, damn, damn.

I didn't even know what to say. I was so angry at her right then for all of a sudden becoming my problem.

But she was so vulnerable and open and alone and raw. It didn't feel right to be the guy I always was with her. But I *had* to be, for her sake. So, fine. We'd skip town and then I'd find her somewhere to go and... We'd cross that bridge when we came to it. For now, I just drove and tried to remember that the girl in the seat was not my girl and though she wanted my comfort, the line was drawn right there.

And I refused to cross it.

FIVE

Dawn broke over the road as we trudged down the highway into the next town. She was asleep in the seat, laid down like a child in the fetal position. I tried to toe the line between speeding and following the law because I knew we needed to get the heck out of dodge, but we also needed to not get pulled over. I imagined Biloxi was behind me somewhere, catching up and right there behind me like he always was. There were four main roads out of that town, and I hope he picked the wrong one and was a hundred miles an hour in the wrong direction.

But since when was luck on my side?

I looked down at Marley and got angry all over again. Now I had this girl to look after. It was always me after my mom died. I never even had an inkling to add someone to the mix. Now when Marley got hurt or killed because of this, I'd have another death on my conscience.

What a friggin' tragedy I'd fallen into. Boy meets girl, girl makes boy question everything for a split second, boy gets girl killed. I didn't like the sound of that. So, though I knew I was being cliché and would ultimately hurt her, I knew what I had to do. I just had to make her see that it was a good idea to get away from me. I could help her get set up somewhere else and then skip town as quickly as I'd come.

Being hated wasn't the hard part. It was living with myself when it was too late.

"One room, please," I spouted. I didn't dare look around the place because I knew the film of gunk and stench would just make me regret stopping. But at $39.99 a night, you couldn't really be picky. We both needed to sleep and get a shower before we started on the road again. I was sure we'd have to start roughing it at some point, but hopefully, she would be gone by then.

"Cash only," the man replied dully and looked at my neck, not my face. "We have too many issues with stolen cards and bank fees."

"That's all I got so that's just perfect, now ain't it?" I handed it to him and wanted to shake my head. It was no secret that these pay-by-the-hour dives were shady and yet they still wanted to keep up the pretense of civility and propriety.

"Here's your key." And it was. The cracked, plastic keychain had the number thirteen on it and from it dangled an old, rusted key.

"Thanks."

"Checkout's at ten, bright and early."

"Swell."

I pushed open the glass door, towing a silent Marley behind me because there was no way I was leaving her alone, and climbed in the truck. We parked in front of our room and went inside. We had no bags, but I'd fix that tomorrow and take her to the nearest Goodwill. The room was all I imagined it would be. Marley was obviously not a frequenter of these types of establishments because she looked around and gasped a little when she saw the ashtray overflowing with butts on the table.

"It's all right," I assured her. "We'll sleep in our clothes and leave first thing in the morning."

I shut the door and went straight to the bathroom. I lifted the shirt off my body, holding in my groan of agony, yanked off the bandage, and got my first good look at the wound. It looked pretty nasty, and although I was skeptical that the hotel water would help in the gangrene department, I stripped out of my pants next and turned the water to scalding.

I'd been in the shower for several long minutes before getting out. My shoulder was pulsing in a bad way and I had nothing for it. I stood there air-drying in that dirty bathroom and wondered what the hell I was going to do. I had my small stash of cash that I always kept on me, but the rest of it was in my apartment. I wondered if it was worth it to go back for it. It was hard enough to take care of myself. A few more days of meals and hotels, and my pockets would be dry.

I threw my clothes back on and came out to tell her we needed to try to save as much as possible and eat something small and cheap tonight, but the room was empty. My breath jammed in my throat. "Marley?" I called out.

When she didn't answer, I bolted to the door and threw it open, only to find a surprised Marley. Her arms were full of bandages, aspirin, and peroxide. She even had two sandwiches and two bottles of apple juice. I yanked her inside and slammed the door shut, bolting it before turning and glaring at that daggum gorgeous girl. She had my ball cap on and her hoodie pulled up. "What the hell are you doing?" I roared.

She leaned away as if taken aback by my response. How could she not understand why I'd be upset? I explained to her that we were being followed, she'd seen with her own gorgeous blue eyes that he'd shot her place up, and she knew we were running and being careful, so why...

"I'm sorry," she whispered. "I thought-"

"What part of *we're on the run* don't you get?"

"I know that, but I was hungry, so I knew you would be, too-"

"I can handle that. You don't ever do that again." I lifted my hands in frustration, my knuckles grazing the cheap ceiling tiles. "I'm at a loss at what the hell to say to you right now. I can't even go take a shower and trust you to sit tight 'cause the second I do, you bolt for a snack?"

My breathing was crazy, the wound on my back aching and pulsing angrily. She looked like I'd struck her. I waited for her to defend herself, and when I finally saw the hardness come over her, I bucked up for a fight. "Wow, you are so jaded, Jude."

"That's nothing new."

"I was just trying to-"

"Just stop."

"You're not the leader of this outfit. I don't know why you think-"

"Enough," I growled, leaning back against the door. I winced as my shoulder protested. "If you're with me, you can't just leave whenever you feel like it. I already have you on my conscience. Let's not add your death to it."

Her chest deflated, like she held a breath to say something and decided against it. She stood there, her sweet face wearing a weary look that hurt my chest.

I looked, really looked, at the stuff in her arms. Dang... It was all stuff for me. She went and got the stuff to re-dress my bandage and the pills out of the truck for me to take. And something to eat. I squinted my eyes shut tight. "Marley, I'm sorry."

"You're right." She looked up at my face. She looked disappointed more than anything else. "Here. This is for you. I won't leave without your *permission* again."

She tossed it all into a heap on the bed and slammed the bathroom door behind her. I turned and bumped my forehead against the door a couple times. I was so out of touch with people that I forgot how to deal with them when I wasn't using them for a purpose.

Wow, what a tool that made me.

I waited for her to come out. I knew knocking wouldn't help. I heard the water running and tried to push the image of her being naked beyond that wooden door out of my mind. I had to remember what I was doing, saving her. I was saving her by keeping her at a distance.

I took my shoes off, but left my socks on, and flopped onto the bed. There were only three channels—one that apparently wasn't friends with the rabbit ears on the TV top. So I watched the news and ate the egg salad sandwich she got me, and then gulped down the juice, too.

She emerged, her blond hair wet and straight. I didn't look away. I wanted her to see that I was sorry. "Sandwich was good. Thanks."

She stared at me for a minute, her shoes in her arms, before finally saying, "You're welcome. I was just trying to help."

"I know," I admitted low and stood. I walked to her and took the shoes from her arms, tossing them in the pile on the floor with mine. "I just don't want anything to happen to you, especially since you're in this mess because of me. Can you imagine what I'd feel if you were hurt and it was all my fault?"

Her face fell a little. "I wasn't looking at it like that. I just thought you needed to rest and I could get back before you got out of the shower."

"I understand," I said. And I did. "I was thinking we could get as far as we could tomorrow and then find you a little place to stay. You can't go back, you know that, right?"

"You're...dropping me off somewhere?" She nodded and turned. "Of course, yeah."

"It's too dangerous to stay with me. Plus, I'm sure you're ready to get your life back to normal."

"Normal," she scoffed. "Homeless is the new normal, right?"

She was still facing the wall.

"I'll get you set up somewhere and then we'll get you a job. It'll be fine. I help you find a home before I leave."

"What about my classes?" She finally turned and I wished she hadn't. Her cheeks were lined with tears, her face full of sorrow. "I worked so hard, sacrificed a place to live, just so I could finish school and find a job that would make it so that I never had to wonder what I was going to eat again. Never not have somewhere to go again. Never have to depend on anyone for anything ever again. You're saying I can't ever go back? That all that time and money spent was...for nothing?"

Oh, no... What had I done? I hadn't just put her in danger, no. No this was way worse. I'd ruined her life. She was right. She could never go back, never transfer to another college with her same name which meant she couldn't transfer her credits. She had to become someone else. He'd find her. All because he'd use her to get to me. All because of me...

"Oh, God...Marley. I'm so sorry."

"Jude," she pleaded, "please don't say that I can't finish school."

"You can't. I'm sorry. I'm more sorry than you'll ever know." I turned with a laugh that was anything but humorous. "See, this is why I don't do people. I can't. They get hurt, they're ruined, they die because of me. If you had never met me, you wouldn't be in this mess right now. You could keep on doing what you were doing, finish school, and never have known anything but your life."

"No," she argued. I didn't turn. "It's not your fault that he's doing this."

"It pretty much is." I looked over my shoulder. "I'm sorry just doesn't quite cover it, but I am sorry."

I stepped into my boots, not even tying them, and went for the door.

"Where are you going?" she asked, panic coating her words.

"Out," I bit out. I knew I was being a jerk, but I needed to get away from her. She was causing me aches and pains in my guts at knowing what I'd done to her, and I wasn't used to caring about...anything. "Stay in the room and lock the door."

"Jude," she protested. "Come on-"

"Stay in the room," I repeated before slamming the door. I waited right there, listening, for her to bolt the latch. When I heard it, I headed downstairs to the bar I'd seen on the way in.

Yep. It was about to be a cliché night all the way around. I was going to get drunker than drunk because I couldn't handle what she was telling me. It was stupid. I was stupid.

I was heartbroken for her, heartbroken that she'd ever had to cross my path.

"Another," I ordered and didn't give a care about the slur. He gave me a look. The look that meant, *You're about to get cut off, buddy.* "Another," I said, harder.

He rolled his eyes and poured the amber liquid into my glass. The bar was a dive of the best kind. Dirty, cheap booze, and nobody cared about what anyone else was doing but themselves. Except the female currently raking my hair. I looked over at her. I hadn't said one word to her, but here she sat, trying to see if she could get lucky with me tonight.

If I wanted to send Marley for the hills, that would be one darn good way to do it.

I shook her hand off and downed my last shot. I felt raw in my insides, but the alcohol was helping the pain in my shoulder. That was a plus. The jukebox was playing country something or other. There was a girl dancing on the bar with short jeans shorts and cowboy boots, like Marley's. A vision of Marley up there doing that dance...

No.

I turned to nameless-girl and smiled. "Hey, darlin'." She beamed. "What are you doing in a place like this?"

"Looking for you, sugar," she said, sweet as saccharin. Her eyes wandered my scar before her fingers did. She made a *Hmm* hum and then purred, "Your scar is pretty hot."

"How about that," I slurred, though my teeth clenched. I felt her hand on my arm and winced when she pulled me.

"Take me to your room," she whispered in my ear. She smelled like vanilla something. I almost shook my head. She was pretty and smelled good, and had no business in a place like this giving herself to any man, just like that. She got closer, pressing her lipglossed lips to my ear. "Take me to your room."

I should do this. I should do it to make sure that Marley didn't have any problems getting the hell away from me when it was time. I should go up there and make a scene so that Marley knew I was a bad guy.

I should do it...

"All right," I drawled. "Let's go."

"You got a tab, pal," the bartender barked.

"I'll get it in the morning."

"You'll get it now."

It was then I remembered how stupid I was. We barely had money for food and now I was drinking the money away. I was becoming a real gem these days. I tossed the money on the bar and heard him grumble about the lack of tip. The girl tossed my arm over her shoulder. I was sure she could see how wasted I was, but I was also sure that she didn't care.

My mind was blank as we made our way to the room. When we stopped at the door was when my brain decided to start working again. I didn't knock. I turned to the girl and opened my mouth to tell her this wasn't going to happen.

As much as I wanted to piss Marley off for her own good so she'd leave, I'd done enough damage tonight. But the door swung open hastily and a worried Marley stepped out...only to step back as if I'd slapped her. Then my lips were being pressed harshly to someone else's and it took a second to realize what was going on. I pushed back a little, but the girl hung on tight before scooting her face along my cheek to my ear and whispering, "You pick up women in bars? Cheaters are bastards. I hope she leaves your sorry behind."

I laughed. "Now, darlin'-"

She leaned back and grinned. "Thanks for that, baby. You want another go-round in the bathroom, you come find me."

Then she sauntered away, fully thinking she'd ruined my relationship with her little infidelity show. I was actually impressed.

But when I looked back at Marley, I wasn't impressed anymore. She had this look on her face....I'd seen it somewhere before. It was right there on the tip of my brain, but wouldn't come. She walked backward into the room and tapped the door almost closed as she went inside. I followed.

"Marley, that wasn't what it looked like."

She chuckled sadly. "What if it was? We're not a couple. I don't care if you bang every skank in this hotel."

"I didn't bang her. I was going to pretend to...or something." My foggy brain was done for the night. "I was bringing her here, but you opened the door before I could tell her no and then she kissed me to get revenge on me for being a cheater."

"What?" she asked. "You're slurring so bad I can't understand you."

"I didn't bang her. I was going-"

"Not this whole spiel again," she groaned. "And will you stop saying *bang her*." She gripped my arm and made me sit on the bed. The room spun and the bed broke my fall. "Wow, you are so drunk." She sounded disappointed. I kept disappointing her. All I wanted to do was protect her, but I kept hurting her. "Let's get your shoes off."

I felt her yank them free and the thud of them hitting the floor.

She leaned over me and I smelled her. That clean, shampoo smell. She touched a spot on my neck and sighed. "Come on," she commanded. "To the bathroom we go."

She threw my arm around her shoulders and we trudged into the dingy bathroom. We stood in front of the mirror, the light blinking with its last breath above us, but even with that, I could still see it. Still see the thing that had made Marley sigh. At some point, nameless-girl must've kissed the side of my neck with her bright red lipstick. There was a clear imprint there. I also had a little on my lips. I leaned on the sink, feeling sick. I turned the water on and put a little soap on my hand, rubbing at the spot and then my mouth.

"Here," she said and handed me a toothbrush with paste on it. She must've bought that while she was out, too. I brushed hard and long. Eventually she took it from me, sat me on the toilet, and helped me take off my shirt. I hated that she was doing this. In my ill attempt to drown my sorrows because of the sorrow I'd caused her, I'd just made things worse.

She looked at my shoulder and hissed. "Oh, my..." She searched around and then ran to the bed and back. "OK, we've got to clean this."

She dabbed, poked, and put things on it. I was too far gone to care or feel it. She taped it all back up and helped me stand. She let me fall gently to the bed.

"You're gonna choke if you throw up." She climbed on the bed with me and tried to push me, to roll me over. She licked her bottom lip in frustration. So I did something epically stupid, but something I very much wanted to do.

And with my inhibitions low, I was apparently going for it.

I pulled her to my chest, my arms around her, and pressed my lips to her neck. I didn't kiss her, just pressed them there.

She was draped across me so I rolled so her legs were on top of us and she was partially under me. I blocked out the spinning room and tried to make her see. I just wanted her to see that I was so broken I didn't even know how to be human anymore. I felt the most raw I ever had and I needed her to see without me saying so that I was a good guy. I wasn't. I wanted her to run...but I wanted her to stay.

"Jude," she whispered and I opened my eyes. She looked confused. "I'm not her. You know that, right? I'm Marley."

I chuckled a little under my breath. "I know exactly who you are," I whispered against her jaw. She took a shuddering breath. I held her tightly, refusing to relinquish her. She didn't fight me and I didn't know why, but I wasn't about to ask.

"I didn't kiss her," I heard myself say, and I wasn't sure why I was supplying the info.

The lamp was on in the corner and I wanted it off, but couldn't move. I drifted. Bits and pieces fought through my mind. Lockers, a school, girls with too much make-up, a girl with a face that could melt hearts, but she was sad. Destroyed...I felt bad for her...

The next thing I knew, the light was winking from the window at me and I felt like my guts were boiling over. Wait, they were...

I bolted to the bathroom, scrambling over the body I was lying next to. I didn't even get to shut the door before I was hugging porcelain. My stomach wretched over and over and over again and then some more. An eternity later, I was sore all over, my head hurt as I laid it against the cool wood of the wall, and I felt too awful to be embarrassed. I heard the water running and then Marley was hunching down, putting the cold cloth on my forehead. I looked at her, knowing there was something that I was supposed to remember.

She watched me. When she licked her bottom lip and sighed, it all rushed back. Me rushing to the bar and spending too much money on alcohol we couldn't afford, bringing the girl back, but changing my mind, her kissing me and hoping I got dumped, Marley taking care of me and then I...I wasn't sure what you called it. I didn't kiss her. No, that other girl had kissed me and I didn't want to taint Marley with that. So I had kissed her neck and jaw instead and then...there we were. Marley and Pukey.

I sighed. "Wow, I'm an ass."

She smiled sadly, the scar on her lip visible and kissable. "Yeah," she agreed.

"I'm so sorry."

"I know."

She gave me the wet rag and I wiped my mouth and face with it. When I looked back at her, I saw the redness of her throat. I stared at in confusion before understanding smacked into me. "Did I do that to you?"

She ran her fingers across it, her lips falling open. "It's nothing."

I touched my jaw. I hadn't shaved in days. "Dang, I can't do anything right, can I?"

"It's all right."

I rubbed my face with my hands. "Bet you can't wait to get away from me. I'm a one man demolition team."

"That's not true," she said, surprisingly forceful. "Will you stop with the pity party this morning?" she spouted and stood. "Come on. Get up. You're buying me breakfast and then we're leaving."

I felt my eyebrows rise. Well...dang. "Yes, ma'am."

I stood with her help and stayed close, looking down at her. Her small hands were on my sides as she attempted to keep me upright. "Are you OK to stand?"

"I'm OK," I told her. "I'm sorry about...everything. And that." I pointed to her neck.

The small smile had more than one meaning. It had my inner guy perking to attention. "Girls don't generally complain about beard burn, do they? Isn't it supposed to be a way for guys to mark girls, claim them, be all romantic in a Neanderthal kinda way, like hickies?"

I arched an eyebrow at her. *Oh, is that right.* She blushed, furiously and adorably, and backtracked.

"I didn't mean you were trying to mark me, I just meant you didn't have to apologize."

I couldn't help myself. I leaned in, putting my hand on the wall behind her head. "How many hickies have you had?"

She licked her bottom lip. Again. "None," she breathed. She put a hand on my chest to keep me from coming closer.

I pursed my lips in approval. "That's a good answer."

"Why do you care?" she asked. It wasn't a demand that she know, it was more like she was genuinely interested. Why did I?

I enjoyed her being that close for a few more seconds before leaning back. "Thanks for taking care of me last night. And for fixing my bandage. I know I was an ass, I'm sorry. I think I owe you some breakfast." I took her hand and towed her to the room. I sat down and tied my boots. When I looked up, she was still standing there, looking a little stunned. "Get your shoes on, sweetheart."

She scoffed, but still smiled as she pulled them on and gathered all our things from the bed. We left in a hurry and I drove us to a place that looked cheap enough for some eggs and bacon.

I couldn't eat and just the smell of bacon made my stomach turn, but I had to let Marley get some food in her. As the sweet, dark coffee made its way down my throat, I stared out the window. Even after what I'd done last night, she still took care of me. Even now, she wasn't angry. I didn't know why. I'd had plenty of female scorn come my way, I was used to it, but she seemed reflective more than mad about everything. I was reflecting on my own.

I realized that Marley reminded me of my mother. Not *like that*, but in the way that they both sacrificed anything and everything for what needed to be done.

She was eating her fruit by hand again, the fork not leaving the table once. Even her French toast she tore into strips and dipped in the syrup. I was so curious about it, but would never ask. I'd never get a chance to where it wouldn't be awkward because I'd never get to know her as much as I wanted to.

The waitress dropped the check at the table wordlessly. I picked it up and pulled my wallet out. All I had left was nine twenties and the bill was fourteen dollars. That didn't leave much left over for lodging and food for later. I cursed myself for my bender that night. It had only been a twenty-five dollar bender, but that was still money that we no longer had.

Marley must have seen my face because she asked, "What's the matter?"

"Just running low on funds," I answered, fully expecting her to throw last night in my face. She didn't.

"I wish I could contribute, but all I have is seven dollars in tips from that night. My shift had just started," she reasoned, like it was all her fault.

"It's not your fault. We'll figure something out. I have five hundred dollars at my apartment. If I knew we could go back and get it..."

"I don't think that's a good idea," she said quickly.

"Me either." I nodded to the waitress to let her know I was ready. "We don't have much left and it's not going to get us very far. We'll have to start pinching pennies."

She nodded while the waitress took the check. We got in the truck and started down the road again, my shoulder aching like a mother, and my mind wondering what the hell we were going to do.

SIX

"Bastard. Mother fan-freaking-tastic. Crap! Crap! Crap! Bastard crap!"

Marley had her mouth covered with her fingers, no doubt disgusted by my outburst. We'd only made it about a hundred and some change down the road before the front driver's side tire blew. I was holding in four-letter words for her benefit, but I was so pissed.

The giggle made me turn. She wasn't horrified; she was laughing at me! "What the hell is so funny?"

"Bastard crap," she said with a grin and giggled again. "I know that whatever is wrong is obviously not good, but...bastard crap?"

I sighed and leaned my head back on the seat, the smile breaking free on my lips. "Oh, boy, you're gonna be trouble, aren't you?" I turned my head on the seat. She just smiled and shrugged one shoulder. One very cute, adorable, sexy shoulder. I shook my head. "All right, I'm going to change the tire. Just sit tight, all right?"

I got out and reached over the truck bed to get the spare...but it was gone. My eyes shot back and forth like it was just hiding and I had somehow missed it. I sighed. Dang, someone had ripped me off. She got out and looked at me expectantly over the truck. "What's wrong?"

"Someone stole the spare."

Her lips parted in surprise. "Oh, no."

"Yeah," I agreed.

"What are we gonna do?"

"Well," I said slowly, raking my hair back. "I'll have to call a tow truck, I guess."

"How much will that be?" she said worriedly.

"Too much," I groaned. I reached in between the seats and hoped that my phone still had some battery left. It was in the red and my charger was at my apartment. I called and explained everything to the guy. He said he had some used tires that I could purchase from him, so we waited in the truck. I played with the radio and then she played with the radio, changing it and laughing when I picked something she didn't like. We started talking about all the places we'd lived. She had moved around a lot, too, but mostly against her will unfortunately from foster home to foster home.

"I've been to fifty different schools, at least. Tons of high schools. Those were the worst to change from one to another. I was always the new kid, never got close to anyone, never had friends because I'd just be leaving again soon," I explained, flashes of schools and nameless faces crossed my mind. It was all a blur.

Her smile changed. "Lots of schools I bet, huh?"

My brow creased in confusion at her mood change. "Yeah. What's wrong?"

"Just…thinking."

Forty-five minutes after my call, a beat-up, red tow truck pulled in behind me. I didn't get a chance to ask her what was wrong before we were climbing into the tow truck and making our way into town. It was a good twenty miles out and when we got there, he said it would be about an hour before he got it all fixed. So, we found a fast food burger place and sat in the back to eat our cheap cheeseburgers.

She told me about her favorite foster home. It was an older lady who would pick her up from school in her wheelchair. They'd walk home together like that every single day. When the state found out the lady could barely walk any longer, they didn't allow her to foster kids anymore and sent Marley to a new home. I saw it all over her face that that old lady was the only place she'd ever been that gave a damn about her. She didn't go into specifics, but I knew she'd been mistreated.

She deserved a better life than one stuck with me.

Whatever town we reached by nightfall was where I planned to drop her off. So after we got the truck back and paid him two thirds of our money for the tow and used tire, we trekked on 'til dark. We were a few hundred miles away from where Biloxi had found me. Hopefully, there would be something I could come up with here for her. I could be pretty crafty when forced.

We hadn't eaten anything since that brunch and after fifty in gas, which we were back to empty already, there was only ten dollars left. So I pulled into the little grocery store, got out, and waited for her to join me because I knew she would. She hopped out and walked beside me inside the harshly lit store. I grabbed a hand basket and went straight for the poor-boy-aisle. I thought about how much money I had left and started putting cans of Vienna sausage in the basket, then a few cans of potted meat and tuna just to mix things up. I grabbed of box of store brand crackers on the way to the register and couldn't believe I hadn't heard one *eew* or anything from Marley.

I paid. This stuff would last us two days, maybe three, but we only had one dollar and thirty-seven cents left, and no hotel money. We'd be roughing it from now on.

I drove us around until I found an old, abandoned gas station and parked us in the back, killing the engine. I opened the bag and took out two cans of Vienna, handing one to her.

"Thanks," she said and popped the top.

"A girl willingly eating Vienna. Now I've seen everything," I joked.

She put one in her mouth and kinda smiled. "It's basically a food group for me."

My smile fell. Crap, I was an idiot. She was living in her car and had said she didn't have much money left after school for food... I shook my head. "Sorry. I forgot that..."

"It's all right." She had devoured her can before I even started mine. "So we're sleeping in the truck, huh?"

"Have to."

She gave a wry grin. "Home sweet home."

"I wish I had never met you."

She stared, unblinking. "What?" she whispered.

"If I had never met you, you wouldn't be eating Vienna sausage while sleeping in my truck."

She laughed a little. "No, I'd be eating Vienna while sleeping in mine."

I felt my eyes bulge. Good Lord, I was such an idiot! If I put my foot in my mouth one more time,

I'd never need to eat again. "I have a thing with you about putting my foot in my mouth."

She reached over and patted my arm. "It's all right, tiger." She grinned. "I forgive you. I'm sure you don't know many people who are home challenged."

"Home challenged," I laughed. "Wow, I've reduced you to making up new phrases just to deal with my stupidity."

"You're not stupid." She sank down further in the seat and put her feet on the dash. She'd taken her shoes off at some point. "So, what's the plan tomorrow?"

I didn't want to talk about it now; I wanted to wait until tomorrow because I knew she'd be upset, but it couldn't be helped. "Well...I think we'll stay here for a bit. Try to get some cash in our hands."

"And how do you expect to do that?"

"I have my ways," I said coyly.

She laughed silently and then said, "I have no doubt in that." I was glad the dark hid my smug grin. "So...do you think those lights will stay on all night?" She looked out the windshield at the street light.

"Probably. Why?"

"I just have a thing about the dark," she said, her voice small. "So...goodnight, then."

"Night, Marley."

She curled up against the door and window. She fidgeted with her pocket and wiped something on her nose. I squinted in confusion for a second, but she seemed normal. I almost thought that she...no. She wouldn't. Besides, we had no money. Where would she get drugs from?

I leaned my head back and was content to sleep in any position, but she kept wrestling with her movements. I realized she probably usually slept in her car's backseat and my old beat-up leather seat wasn't very comfy. So I pulled her by the arm to lay against my side. She didn't protest a lick, which meant she was super tired. Or at least I assumed that's what it meant. It was colder at night and I hoped she wouldn't be too cold.

When she finally went to sleep, I felt like I could, too.

She woke first and woke me up in the process. She must've been wiping slobber off her lip because she hid her face from me as she fixed something. It made me want to chuckle. "Breakfast?"

She reached and held up a can of tuna. "Of champions."

I laughed out loud at that. "You got it."

"So what's your big idea for today?" she asked while picking up bites of tuna from the can by pinching it with her fingers.

"I'll show you. Eat up."

Later, as we drove over to the docks and got out, I searched for my target.

"Great, now I'm gonna smell fishy all day from that tuna," she complained.

"No, not from the tuna," I told her playfully. I pointed to the big boat just coming in. "But you will from that."

"What is that?"

"That's our meal ticket. And hotel ticket if we play our cards right."

She shook her head skeptically. "I've never had a good poker face, Jude. Will we need to lie?"

"Not a lick. This is all brute force and skill." I started to walk toward them, but looked back at her and grinned. "And puppy dog eyes, of course."

She scrambled to catch up. "You're making puppy dog eyes?"

"You are, sweetheart. We need these men to let us work for them for the day. I used to live this way. Find odd jobs, people who just needed something done for a day or two and it was always enough to get me by. So work your magic."

"I'm not a magician." She looked like she was about to throw up. "I'm not good at this kinda thing."

"Work the fish dock often, do you?"

She gave me a dull look. "You are becoming impossible. Why can't you just do it?"

"All right." I agreed because I knew she'd see.

"Excuse me," I called and leaned on the dock rope. "Need any help for the day?"

"Nah, not today, kid."

I looked back at Marley in a *See?* manor. I whispered, "Showtime."

She was agitated, but it probably worked in our favor. "Excuse me. I'm sorry." They both looked over in annoyance, but I saw the softness come over them. It was hilarious how gullible men were. Freaking hilarious. "Look, we haven't had a meal in a day. We slept in our truck last night and don't know what we're going to do tonight either. We're not looking for a handout, just to work for what we earn. Do you have anything we can do for some extra cash?"

And puppy dog eyes ensued. Bingo.

"Aw, come on, Mike," one of the guys said to the other.

He sighed, but smiled at her. Not me, her. "All right, honey. Hope you're ready to work."

Honey? I felt my scowl.

"We are," she assured and took my arm, towing me as she followed them down the dock.

They had us weighing fish, then cutting off the heads and measuring crabs. Not once did Marley act disgusted or grossed out. She never complained, never whined. That girl worked her adorable butt off. The sun was starting to beat down on us, even though it was fall. The ache in my shoulder was starting to feel different and not in a good way. It felt deep, all the way to my bones. I tossed my wife beater off to give it some air, figuring the heat from the sun might help. It didn't, but I had to keep working so we'd get our loot for our day of work.

They even gave us a ham sandwich at lunchtime before putting us right back to work. She started to hum as we boxed up the fish and labeled them before throwing them on the ice truck. It was fascinating, but I tried not to stare at her. I had already broken several of my rules with her and needed to remember that the end goal was to get her to leave.

We worked all day and at almost sundown, they gave us a hundred and fifty dollars in cash to split. Not a gold mine in the least, but it would mean we'd eat real food tomorrow. We thanked them for their help. As we walked back to the truck, I started to suggest we sleep in it again to save money, but we both reeked of fish. No way out of it. We had to get a hotel and shower or no one would hire us tomorrow for sure.

This room was better than the last if you discounted the fact that the clerk looked like the guy from Psycho. Marley bolted in the room and squealed, "Dibs on the shower!"

I chuckled and wondered about dinner. We really should stick to the Vienna, but you couldn't eat that non-stop. We worked hard today and I really didn't want to go out anyway. My stomach was presently trying to eat itself.

I searched for a phone book, groaning as I went from the ache making its way from my shoulder down my arm, and found a coupon in the yellow pages for a pizza place, so I tore it out and called. They said they'd be there in thirty minutes or it was free. I begged for them to take longer than that. Free pizza couldn't hurt right now.

She was out of the shower in five minutes flat and came out. My heart jammed itself in my throat. She held her hand up to stop my protest. *As if* I'd protest her naked in a towel. "We have to wash our clothes, Jude. They smelled fishy."

Dang. We ran out of money before we could get to the Goodwill to buy some used ones. "Right. No problem."

She crawled under the covers carefully, pulling the comforter up to her neck. So daggum adorable.... The universe hated me. The guy said there was only one-bed rooms left and now I had to sleep next to her with nothing but towels on.

"I ordered pizza. It was really cheap."

She sighed in relief. "Good. I was hoping we wouldn't eat canned bits-n-pieces tonight. I'm starving."

I laughed slightly as I went to grab a quick shower. I wanted to be out before the pizza guy came. I scrubbed and scrubbed, but tried not to mess with my shoulder. It was hurting something awful and had begun to pulse. I didn't know what to do for it. So I used the soap to wash my clothes in the sink as best I could and hung them on the towel rack with Marley's. Hopefully, they'd be dry in the morning.

I wrapped the towel around my hips and opened the door slowly. Marley was huddled under the covers, the TV on the Home Improvement channel, and she wouldn't look at me. I even walked in front of the TV to get to my side of the bed, but her eyes never left it. Like she was forcing them to stay.

Then, like an idiot, I wondered if she'd ever been with a guy before. She said she'd never had a hickie, but that didn't mean anything. I wanted to kick myself for hoping that she hadn't. Why did the guy in me want to keep this girl when my rational side knew this was a bad idea?

I leaned my head back against the headboard and shifted so my shoulder wasn't pressing on it, too. She finally looked at me. "Oh, no. Your shoulder hurting you?"

"Yes," I answered, my eyes closed.

"I have the aspirin here." She pushed back the covers and went to the plastic bag that held all we had left in the world and got it, shaking four of the pills into her hand. Then she gave me a glass of water from the bathroom. "Here. I'll clean it again for you later."

"Thanks." I downed them and leaned back again, trying not to go to sleep before the pizza arrived. When the knock sounded, I held my hand up letting her know I'd get it. I took fifteen dollars, opened the door, took the two large pizzas from him, and shoved the money at him. "Keep the change."

I slammed the door and bolted it. I heard him through the fiberglass door. "Keep the change? You only gave me ninety-two cents, douche."

"Take it or leave it, buddy!" I called.

"Thanks a lot, freak. Who answers the door in a towel?" He kicked the door before walking away.

Marley and I looked at each other and laughed. She kept giggling and it was contagious. I kept laughing and then she laughed harder. Finally, we settled and ate our pizza with no plates. She folded hers in half the long way and dug in. She plowed through five slices like I'd never seen a girl do. It was pretty awesome.

We tried to watch some TV, but we were pretty exhausted. I flipped it off, turned on my side that wasn't hurting, and tried to pretend that my arm wasn't aching like something was seriously wrong. My eyes closed, but my mind didn't stop. I waited for her to come out of the bathroom, and when she did, I went in. When I came out, I could see her in the light streaming in from the open bathroom door. She was messing with her nose again, like in the truck.

I saw red.

I took off in a stomp toward her, forgetting all about my aching shoulder. I couldn't believe what I was seeing. How dare she snort whatever the hell she was snorting in the predicament we were in? Where had she even gotten it from?

I slammed the bathroom door, but it bounced back, shutting us to almost darkness. Climbing over the bed hastily on my knees, I yanked her over to lay flat on her back. "What the hell do you think you're doing?"

She gasped and tried to fight me so I couldn't see. "Get off me!"

"Why? Show me what you got, Marley," I taunted in anger. "Maybe I want some, too."

"Get off me!" she screeched. It sounded haunted and terrified.

I finally got her flat on her back, her hands over her head held by mine, my face right in hers. "What the hell, Marley?"

"Get off me," she said, her voice crumpling. "Get off, get off, get off!" Her legs scissored under me, trying to move them to the side.

I loosened my grip a little and hated that she had so much control over me. She started to whimper and confusion ran through my blood. She moved her legs to the side and turned her face away... A repulsive thought flitted through my mind... Her in foster homes, so many of them, so many men she must've come into contact with... She was acting as if I were about to hurt her or....something way worse than that...

I jumped off her as quickly as I could and didn't stop until my back slammed into the wall. It jarred the bathroom door open a little with the impact and I groaned at the rage of pain through my shoulder. I gripped my arm and tried to breathe through my nose to stave off my rush of breaths making the pain worse.

I saw her through the crack of light covering her body on the bed. She had scrambled up to the headboard, her knees to her chest, and was looking at me with a mix of horrified terror and sympathy.

Her breaths were loud and ragged as she watched me. I slid to the floor, but could still see her over the bed.

"I'm sorry I...scared you," I said because I didn't know what *to say*.

"It was dark," she admitted after a couple minutes of silence. "And you jumped on me. Why?"

"This is the second time I've caught you snorting," I said evenly. "I couldn't let it go this time."

"Snorting?" Her brow creased, her cheeks still red. "Coke?" She said incredulously. "Cocaine? You thought I was snorting cocaine?"

"What were you doing?"

She held something up in the light. It was a small wrapper that kind of looked like a Band-Aid. She pulled what was behind it out and I saw a small butterfly bandage looking thing.

"It's a nose strip. Jackass."

Nose strip? "What do you use those for?"

"To breathe, obviously."

"You got a cold or something?"

She shook her head slowly but angrily. "No, I don't have a cold." She seared me with her gaze. "The foster dad who raped me also broke my nose. I have a deviated septum and have never been able to get it fixed. There. Now you know all my little secrets. Poor Marley." She choked on a sob, switching gears faster than I could keep up. "Poor Marley's homeless and can't be in the dark because she has nightmares about an ass that used to come in her bedroom. And she has to steal nose strips from pharmacies when they stop to get supplies because she can't afford them otherwise and she can't sleep well without them. Poor Marley doesn't eat with forks because she doesn't have any and she's so used to eating without it that she doesn't feel right using them. There, Jude. All my crap's on the table now."

She got up and went into the bathroom. She didn't slam the door, which surprised me. It closed gently behind her and I felt like a bastard through and through as I listened to her soft mewls through the door. She didn't come out for a long time. I knew she wouldn't so I propped myself up on it and lay there all night. If she wasn't getting a good night's sleep on the bed, then I wasn't either.

SEVEN

I paced the room slowly for a long time before opening the bathroom door, knocking softly first. No answer. It was so hot in the room that morning, but the air conditioning was on full blast. When I pushed the door open, she was lying in the tub, using a towel as a pillow. She was awake and looked up at me. She was no longer angry, but she didn't look normal either.

I sat down on the floor beside the tub opposite her head, careful to keep the towel around my hips secure. We stared at each other. My eyes felt hot and strange, but I stared back. Minutes passed before I finally spoke. "Life sucks, Marley."

Her eyes widened for a second before her lips twitched, begging to release a smile. "Yeah, sometimes."

"Pretty much all the time," I countered.

"You're so jaded, Jude," she repeated what she'd said the other night. I guess it was pretty true.

I nodded. "It appears that way."

She gripped the edge of the tub as if hanging on to keep from falling and swallowed. "I've never told anyone about what happened to me when I was younger. I've never had someone to tell before. I've never *wanted* to tell anyone before."

I scoffed. "I doubt you wanted to tell me either." I shook my head. "I'm sorry I forced that out of you."

"But you didn't. If I hadn't wanted to tell you, I wouldn't have."

I felt a little spark hit me, like a ray of sunshine right to my heart. She *wanted* to tell me, to trust me with something like that?

"Why me? Why me when I was being a jerk?"

She sighed. "You thought I was doing something awful. I get that. I'm sorry, I'm just so broken I don't even know how to be a real human being anymore."

I stared at her. I had said that exact same thing about myself. This felt like more than some fluke. This felt like a path was thrown in front of us and we could either take it or walk away. We both had learned to live a normal life—what was normal for us. Even though our lives weren't ideal, and we may not be the most pleasant people in the world, we survived.

And that was the point.

"You're human," I said, my voice deep and meaningful with my revelation. "And you are beautiful, and it's more than just your face. You took care of me even after knowing that I'd taken everything from you." Her face scrunched in question. "I'm sorry. I'm sorry about everything you had to go through to get here."

"I just wish I could be normal. Not be scared, not be scarred." She touched her lip and I wanted to pull her to me, but I didn't. "I got this from another foster parent. The mom caught me sneaking out and hit me. I fell into the window pane."

My heart stopped. "Gah...Marley."

"I'm not telling you this to make you feel sorry for me...Really, truly, I'm over it all for the most part. The...rape. It was one time and he was so drunk that he didn't even remember it. I don't think about it anymore...unless it's dark. I have more issues with this," she touched her scarred lip, "to be honest. I just feel like..." She leaned a little closer and opened up her very soul. She looked as raw as I felt. "I feel like you may not know exactly what I'm going through, but you're still right there with me on your own. We're both paddling against the current, just trying to catch up, just trying to simulate some sense of normalcy...though neither of us are normal."

I leaned forward, too, and let my hand rest on her arm. I moved my thumb back and forth over her wrist, marveling at how incredibly soft her skin was in that spot. "You have to take the things that happened to you and push it all toward something else. We have to take those things, those awful things, and make our lives better because we lived through it."

Her eyes glistened, but she smiled a little. I wanted to kiss that scar so badly. "Like beauty from ashes?"

"Exactly like that." It was so warm in there. The air conditioning must've been broken. My shoulder pulsed with each heartbeat and my eyes were so hot they burned. "You and me, Marley, we're going to be all right one day."

She put her hand over mine on her arm. Her smile changed and she leaned a little closer. "Are you all right? You have sick eyes."

"Sick eyes?"

"It's what one of my foster moms used to say. It's what your eyes look like when you're sick, when you have a fever."

"I'm fine," I reassured her.

"You're pretty hot, Jude," she remarked, running her palm up my arm. "Are you sure you're all right?"

"Yeah." I stood and stretched, but immediately regretted it.

"Your arm," she hissed. "I didn't clean it last night. I'm sorry. Hold on."

She stood and ran to get the aspirin. "It's freezing in here," she said, rubbing at her arm. It wasn't cold, it was blazing in there, but I didn't argue.

Then she spent the next ten minutes being extra careful and gentle while she fixed me up. The towel was securely under her arms and above her chest. Her extremely nice chest that was right in my line of sight as I sat on the toilet. Her soft, lean arms that brushed my face several times during her ministrations as she stood between my knees. It was the time that her chest brushed my face that killed me. I groaned—totally not my fault—and she stopped dead. "Oh, my gosh. I'm so sorry."

I chuckled and looked up at her with a grin that wouldn't stop. "Are you really apologizing? Come on, it was the highlight of my week."

She shook her head, but smiled. "Wow, the male species has seriously declined."

"Guilty," I admitted. "I live on the four basic food groups. Meat, sweet tea, a place to sleep, and a pretty girl."

Her face changed to that sad one that kept coming back no matter what I did. "Yeah," she said softly.

"What's the matter?"

"Nothing." She put the last piece of tape on and leaned back. "I can just imagine that you get lots of girls."

"I did," I answered truthfully. "Honestly...it's not all it's cracked up to be."

"But I bet you used to really enjoy it, right?" she asked harder. "I bet you used to just eat up all that attention."

I scowled. "What's going on?"

"Nothing."

"Are you jealous?" I asked, but as soon as it left my lips, I knew I was an idiot.

She scoffed. "I think we'd have to be together for me to have something to be jealous about first. Secondly, no, not jealous, I just used to know a jerk *exactly like you*. And he loved it."

I stood, thinking that I wasn't sure if I believed her or not. Her being jealous would be sexy as all get out.

"That's not true. You can be jealous even when the person doesn't belong to you." I wiped at my forehead and wasn't surprised by how much I was sweating. "And you kind of sound jealous."

"I'm not jealous," she spouted and tacked on a head shake. "I'm not interested in being with a guy that can be with any woman, anytime, anywhere and it doesn't even faze him. For someone to be so uncaring, so unattached, doesn't appeal to me in the slightest. Someone that doesn't care about anything but his current conquest..."

"What makes you think that I'm that way?"

She laughed humorlessly. "Well, for one, you brought a freaking girl back to bang in the hotel room that I was in with you. I had nowhere to go for this little tryst, since you won't let me go anywhere without you, so what were you going to do with me, huh? Stick me in the bathroom?"

"I hadn't thought that far," I muttered to myself. Her eyes widened. "Look, I'm sorry about that. I wasn't really going to have sex with her, I was just...trying to prove a point."

"A point? What, that you're an ass? I already knew that."

My jaw tightened, but I knew I deserved it. "I'm sorry, Marley. I've done some things in my life that I'm not proud of. We just talked about taking the things in our life and giving them new life and purpose somewhere else, to push it into another direction to make us better people?" I sighed. "I don't like who I used to be. I want to be different."

She looked away. "Can I just ask why?" She looked back at me. "Why you would bring a girl back here with you?"

Honesty is the best policy, right? "I was trying to make you angry, make you hate me."

She pulled her clothes from the towel rack and turned to glare at me. "That's the dumbest thing I've ever heard. Get dressed. We need to get to the docks and see if I can sweet-talk another day of work outta them or else this crappy hotel won't last long."

She slammed the door, leaving me feeling like a tornado just went through. She yelled through the door, "And don't you even think about coming out without knocking!"

"Yep."

I got dressed in a stupor. The fever was lessened, but I still felt it raging in my arm. When I knocked and came out, she was sitting, her knees to her chest by the door. "Ready?"

She glanced up. "Always."

The fishermen let us work that day and the next three for the same amount of money each day, but said they'd be heading to the next port and wouldn't need us anymore. So we'd have to find more odd jobs elsewhere. Marley was quieter than normal, but we were both so tired and exhausted when we got back that we didn't really have time to talk anyway.

I had started to reconsider my leaving her there in that town, but with this recent shift in our 'relationship', it was unclear. I thought we'd made this breakthrough and then she...blocked everything out and hid inside herself.

When I got out of the shower that night, Marley wasn't in the room. I freaked and ran, looking under the beds, closets, and out the door. I shut it and gripped my forehead in anger. They'd taken her from the room? I hadn't heard anything. I jerked my shoes on to go after them, somehow, but saw a note on the bed.

Went to the bar. Had to get out of this room. Maybe I'll make a few bucks while I'm there, too.

Mother... I ran out the door to the bar downstairs. I opened the door, bypassed the bouncer who could give a crap, and then gripped the doorframe at what I saw. Marley was there, her short shorts and cowboy boots on as she sat on the bar. She waited for the bartender to fill up the tray and then hopped down, carrying it to a group of eager guys by the pool tables. "Now," she said and passed them around, "double or nothing, boys."

My teeth ground together. She was betting our money? But then guilt rose up. Hadn't I been in a bar just a few nights before spending it on booze? I grabbed a water from the bar and then watched her from the room, moving from one side to the other. My arm ached, radiating pain and making it hard to breathe. Making me want to get a shot just to calm down the pain, but I'd made enough of an ass of myself that night.

She watched, a pool stick in her hands, as one of them lined up his shot. She bit into her lip and then yelled, "Come on, Pablo! You got this."

He grinned at her and missed his shot. She bounced and giggled before setting up her own. I growled under my breath at the way she bent over the pool table. There wasn't a dude in the place not staring at that behind.

She sunk her striped three ball in the corner pocket. She squealed and they laughed and huffed, willing to lose to her. She watched another go round with the four guys playing, doing all the right things at the right times to make them lose, and then she sunk her seven ball.

Holy crap. She was hustling them.

I never knew if she saw me or not, but once the game was over, they paid her some amount I didn't know and she hugged them all and laughed loudly. It almost looked like she was drunk.

I knew that she wasn't though.

They all left, but there was still plenty of people in the bar. She went to the jukebox, much like my boss had that day, and put her dollars in, selecting a song that she loved, and started to dance.

She was a siren sucking me into her web because I couldn't look away. I was mesmerized at how incredibly sexy she was. Her eyes were closed, her hips moved to their own rhythm. I was so pissed at her for leaving, so worried about her, so freaking turned on.

She danced right there, the angle perfect for my viewing. She turned and gave me a show, almost like she knew...I was there.

I scowled. She was hustling *me*, too.

Daggumit.

I stood, the stool creaking across the floor causing her eyes to open. She didn't seem surprised to see me there. I gave her a look to let her know I was pissed. She didn't smile, she just kept dancing, turning away from me.

When the song was over, she moved on to something else. She joked with the guys playing darts, she even took a few orders and brought them their drinks, happily accepting their tips with a little shoulder shrug and a smile.

I'd had my fill and wasn't about to stand there and watch anymore. I willed her to look at me, taking the last sip of my water, and when she did, I jerked my head toward the door. She looked like she wanted to protest, but obliged me by moving slowly toward me.

"Did you enjoy yourself?" I said harshly, though I had no right to.

"I did actually." She turned on the stairs up to our room and handed me a wad of folded cash. "There's one-fifty there. You're welcome."

I scoffed and watched the back of her jeans as we went upstairs. "There are better ways to do it."

"I needed to get away from you." She looked at me as I unlocked the door. "And this room. All of it."

"Away from me, huh?" My bitterness was growing. She hated me. I had accomplished that. And now, I wasn't even sure if that was what I wanted.

"Yes," she answered and flipped her boots off her feet before putting her nose strip on, still not letting me see it, and then climbing up to her pillow. She lay down on her stomach. "It's obvious you can't wait to dump me off." Her voice was muffled. "It really sucks to be around someone who doesn't even want to talk to you."

Had I given her that impression? I thought she hadn't wanted to talk to me. "I do want you around," I heard myself say. I scowled at myself. "I thought you were angry with me."

"I was. I am." She looked at me from under her hair. "We don't just never speak again because I got mad at you."

"Well," I stalled, "you didn't speak to me either." I climbed into bed, faced away from her, and hated the whole situation. "And for the record, I would never have asked you to bar hustle for money. You could've gotten hurt."

She was silent for a while. I thought she was asleep, when I heard her. "Is that the only reason?" she asked in a whisper.

I let it go and didn't say a word.

I woke sometime later in the middle of the night to the screams of a banshee. I sat up swiftly, looking around for Biloxi or someone in the room. Marley was standing in the one chair provided in the hotel, pointing and screaming at something.

"For the love of all, what's the matter with you?"

"There! It's right there." I looked and behind the bed on the wall was a huge cockroach. The bathroom light showed just enough for me to see it. I got all the way up as she kept screaming. "Oh, my gosh. It touched me!" She shivered and shifted her legs back and forth. "It was crawling on my neck. Oh, my gosh, please kill it."

I rubbed my eyes, feeling the uncomfortable heat behind them, and grabbed my shoe. When I came for it, it ran, on its way to the window. I bolted and smashed it with the sole of my shoe on the wall by the air conditioner. I tossed the shoe in the corner and curled back up in the covers. I heard her mumbling, 'Gross' and 'Oh, my gosh. Oh, my gosh.'

She crawled into the bed with me and scissored her legs under the sheet for a few minutes. I could tell she was working up the nerve to ask me something, I just didn't know what. Then she leaned over and wrapped her arm around my waist. "Please, please let me snuggle with you. Please. There could be more bugs here," she whispered into my neck and shivered. "Jude, please."

I sighed and rolled over, opening my arm to her. She put her cheek to my chest and I figured it was an opportune time to touch her since she was asking for it. I let my hand pull her closer and rubbed her arm. She was asleep in no time. My shoulder ached to lay on it, but I wasn't about to move for anything in this world.

The next morning, I was alone in the bed. As I waited for her to get out of the bathroom so we could go to the thrift shop and then go see about some work, I was numb. My brain refused to work properly. I was so tired and so achy like I'd stayed up all night, but I had slept. I had to lay on my stomach last night because my shoulder just hurt too badly. Even though she cleaned and bandaged it every night, it wasn't doing any good.

I was starting to worry about it. I couldn't go to the doctor for it. Couldn't risk being put into the system and having to move again so soon. Even though I'd fallen asleep early last night, I was fighting sleep again. It was freezing in the room, but my arm was so hot. It was an uncomfortable combination. My head pulsed with every noise.

She came out, but I couldn't move. I waited there under the covers until I felt her cool fingers touch my forehead. It was like a dream. I could feel her, but couldn't move or talk. My head turned to the side when she let go and I began to shiver. Everything blurred, nothing seeped through, nothing mattered. It was like being high in a really bad way. And my shoulder no longer just hurt, it was excruciating.

I wanted to rub it, but my arm wouldn't move. I felt lips on my ear and heard in the softest whisper, "Just hold on. Jude, you *better* hold on."

I felt movement and heard the door open and close, and then an engine rumble and bright lights coming and going back into darkness. And then nothing.

EIGHT

Beeping and a soft hand on my cheek woke me. I squinted hard as all my senses opened up at once. "I know the light's bright. I'm sorry, but we have to go," she hissed.

Marley.

My eyes opened and I looked at her above me. She looked worried and tired. "What's the matter, sweetheart?"

She sighed and smiled in exasperation. "Good Lord, do not try to pick me up right now." She pulled my good arm until I was sitting. I was groggy and nauseous. "Sorry. Gotta get dressed. We need to go."

"Where am I?" I asked, even as I looked around the room. It was a hospital room. I looked back at her in panic. "We can't be here."

"Duh, I'm trying to get you out of here."

"How long have I been here?" She pulled the shirt over my head and yanked the gown off in one pull. "The better question is why am I here?"

"You had an infection," she said slowly, helping me with my pants and socks. "In your shoulder. It was spreading to your heart. Your fever was a hundred and five when we brought you in."

We? "Who's we?"

"The guy staying in the room next to ours. I yelled for help because I couldn't carry you and didn't want to call an ambulance unless I had to. He came running over and helped me get you here."

She slipped my shoes on, kneeling at my feet, and stood me up. "You think you can get that?" She nodded to my fly.

"Yeah," I said gruffly and did the button. "How long have I been here?" I repeated.

"About eleven hours." She held her hand up to stop me. "They don't know your name. I told them I didn't know you so they would just check you in as a John Doe and treat you. Then, after the shift change, I came back here to see you. I wanted to wait as long as I could, hoping they'd change the IV bag with antibiotics before we had to take off so you'd get at least two doses of it. You may have even gotten three, not sure. She just changed it a few minutes ago, so we need to scram." She unhooked the bag from the IV pole and got me to hold it in my good arm. "We'll leave the IV in and you can finish the antibiotics and pain meds in the bag at the hotel." She rummaged through some drawers and put bandages and tape in her pocket. "I just hope and pray that it's enough antibiotics to make you better."

I huffed a surprised breath. "You did all this? You concocted this plan all by yourself?"

"Hey, now," she complained in jest.

"I didn't mean it like that."

"I'm good under pressure," she explained with a smile. "Let's go. Truck's outside."

"How did it get here?"

"He drove it and parked it. I parked his in the ambulance bay so I could get you out quick and he picked it up there last night."

"Dang, girl..." I laughed under my breath. "You thought of everything."

"They don't know who you are," she reassured as she peeked out of my room door and we started down the hall. "The hospital. You're safe. He won't find us here."

"Thank you," I said, my words sincere. "I can't believe how much better I feel already."

"I'm so glad," she said on a sigh of relief. "I was so worried that it was all for nothing and you'd still feel awful."

She was worried. I hated that she was worried about me...wasn't I? "Thank you."

"No problem."

"This is the second time you've taken care of me."

"You saved my life," she rebutted. "I think the ratio is one life-saving to three take-care-ofs."

I smiled and walked a little faster to help her out as much as I could. "OK. If you say so."

She drove and picked up some soup on the way to the hotel. I was shocked at how sexy it was for her to be driving my big, ugly, beat-up truck. She handled it like a pro.

I carried my IV inside and sat against the headboard, kicking my shoes off. She opened the lid of Chic-Fil-A chicken noodle soup and handed it to me. It was the best meal I'd had in days. I moaned as it went down. She giggled at me and sat in the chair next to the bed. After I was done, I laid back and tried to watch CSI. Marley kept glancing my way though, and it distracted me.

"I'm OK," I told her.

"I'm just worried that it wasn't enough." Her voice was soft and...scared.

"I feel better."

"You didn't see yourself," she whispered. "You didn't see how bad you were. I thought..." she gulped, "I thought it was over. I really thought you might not make it. You were so hot and you wouldn't wake up and..."

"I'm OK," I repeated with more emphasis. "I promise. I'll tell you if anything feels out of whack."

She nodded her approval.

I sighed. "I'm sorry about our last conversation."

"It's fine. As long as it's not *our last* conversation, then it'll be all right," she replied and smiled, leaning over to tap my arm with the side of her fist. "You worried the crap outta me."

I smirked as much as I could. "Forgive me?"

"Maybe," she spouted coyly. "I think you have some making up to do."

"Making out? What?" I teased.

"Up. Making up, you perv," she laughed her words. "Insufferable pig."

I felt a spark in my chest, a ray of sunshine making its way in. "Wow, I missed you."

She laughed louder. "You didn't even know where you were! You did not miss me."

Then it all just stopped being playful. "But I did, Marley. I did miss you."

Her face said that she understood the meaning and her eyes turned glassy before she climbed over me onto the bed, curling up against my good arm. "I'm really glad you're all right."

I pulled it around her, encouraging her to burrow in. "I'm really glad you're here."

I felt her smile against my shirt front. "I'm glad you're glad."

The rest of the night was spent with the IV bag rigged with a hotel pen and tape to the bedpost and us watching cop shows all night until we fell asleep. And she stayed right there all night, only leaving for a minute to get a nose strip from our plastic grocery bag. She didn't seem as self-conscious this time, but still hid her face in my chest.

I didn't know who fell out first, but we both slept there together, my arm around her, her arm around me, and for once in my life, I didn't feel like everything I touched turned to dust.

The knock on the door woke me. My arm burned and I looked down to find blood coming from my hand into the IV wire. The IV bag was empty. The knock sounded again, waking Marley. She lifted and wiped under her eyes. "Someone knocking?" she said in annoyance.

"Yeah," I told her, smiling at her.

"I got it," she spouted, her voice husky from morning time, and looked through the peephole. "Oh, it's our neighbor."

She opened the door and it revealed a big guy, his arms the size of melons. He was almost bald with his short, shorn hair. I started to peel the tape off my arm and gently pulled the needle out. Blood started coming fast. I cursed and Marley turned.

"Jude, you've got to put pressure on it for a minute," she chastised and ran to get the gauze she'd stolen from the hospital.

She knelt down in front of me and pressed the gauze to my skin. Then she cleaned the blood up and taped it, ripping pieces of tape with her teeth. I watched the guy, who still stood at the door, with skepticism. He hadn't taken his eyes from Marley the entire time. His eyes were currently on her magnificent backside. I knew that backside didn't belong to me, but it might very soon. But it didn't belong to him either.

After last night and what she did for me yesterday, I didn't know what I wanted anymore. I didn't want her to get hurt, I knew that, but I wanted to keep her. I felt selfish, but it also felt wrong to just throw her into the world and hope that Biloxi didn't find her.

But right then, nothing mattered but this jackhole who was about to get kicked in the teeth. "Hey, buddy. Eyes up top, why don't ya?"

She gasped, but I was staring down the neighbor. I saw her in my peripheral as she looked up at me before looking back at him. He tried to look shocked, but I knew better. "Jude," she said low.

I looked at her and her cheeks were red with embarrassment. She was really mad at *me* in this scenario? "He was straight up looking at your-"

"OK, OK," she said in a hiss. She stood, turning to him. "Um..."

He rubbed his nonexistent hair. "I was just checking to see how he was doing, making sure you got back all right."

Oh, please.... "Yep, we made it just fine. Marley is an incredible girl that doesn't need anybody's help." Maybe that was overkill.

She gave me a look that begged me to stop. She took a step toward him and my blood chilled. "I'm sorry," I heard her say in a low voice. "It's been a rough few days for us."

"I can imagine," he agreed and smiled. He put his arm up in the doorframe. "Well, I can take you to get some lunch if you like and we can bring him back some soup or something."

My eyes bulged. Hell no.

I stood, walked forward, making sure my strides were strong and tall, and went to her side. "I'm perfectly fine today. It was just an infection in this nasty cut I had. Thanks for the invite, but we've got some shopping and things to do today before we hit the road."

He seemed surprised. "You're leaving?" he asked her.

"Um..." she looked at me, "we were just passing through so, yeah."

"Oh." He cleared his throat. "OK. Well, holler if you need anything until then. Glad you're doing OK, buddy."

"Thanks...buddy."

He left without shutting the door. She turned to look at me.

"Holler?" I scoffed. I waited to meet her gaze, knowing she was going to be furious with me for acting like I owned her, but when I finally looked over, she looked confused. "Don't look so bewildered, sweetheart. You're too daggum cute for your own good."

She rolled her eyes. "Shopping? Jude, you can't go shopping today. You were just in the hospital yesterday!"

"I feel fine. I feel great actually. A little tired maybe, but we can't just sit in the hotel for days and days waiting for me to be tip-top again. I'm good to go."

"Shopping for what?" she said in concession.

"Well," I drawled and took the corner of her shirt between my fingers. "We need some clothes, don't we?"

She took a deep breath. "Yeah."

"So, that's what I'm doing today. I'm going to get you those clothes I promised you."

She looked at the floor. "Before you take me to the next town and dump me off, right?"

I opened my mouth to tell her that wasn't happening, but closed it. I wanted her to stay with me, I did, I just didn't know what was best. How far would he go to find me? Would he just keep searching for me, or if he didn't find me, would he go in search of Marley?

So I just said the truth. It was actually pretty liberating not to have to blow smoke all the time. "I don't want to leave you anywhere, darlin'."

She winced. "Please don't call me darlin'." I felt my brow bunch in confusion. "That's what you call girls when you're trying to placate them. Makes them feel special, but really it's a decoy move."

I felt my eyebrows rise that she had figured things out like that. "If I recall, I've only ever called you darlin' once before now. Just then was a slip-up. You've been sweetheart since that day in the bar."

"And I'm perfectly fine with it staying sweetheart," she whispered, looking dazed.

I groaned inside. "If we're opening this can and being completely honest, I want to keep you with me. You..." Her eyes begged me to say something romantic and epic. She wanted this, too? Wanted me? I thought she just didn't want to be alone. "You make this life bearable." She closed her eyes for a few too-long seconds. "You're changing me, in all the ways I thought were dead and long gone. I thought I could never be more than I used to be, but you showed me that I can. That I want to be."

She didn't nod, but I could see her hopefulness on her face. But I had to tell the truth. "But I just don't know if the safest place for you is with me."

She didn't deflate like I thought she would. She smiled and stepped forward, touching my cheek. "I'm so glad you're OK. Let's go get some clothes first, and then some lunch second, and then we'll figure out what to do next. OK?"

I nodded. I was going to kiss her if she didn't... She pulled away to put her shoes on and I sighed. She had been so close to getting the kiss of her life. God, help me...did you send her to me? Because it felt like you did. It felt like you put her on this earth to find me and take over my very being with her goodness. I closed my eyes and hoped so.

"Shoes, Jude. I'm starving!" she taunted and put her hands on her hips. "Let's go. I think you surviving your bout of death on a platter deserves something—like a steak with mashed potatoes and yeast rolls."

I chuckled. "You got it, sweetheart."

All that morning, as I we looked around the Goodwill for clothes and jackets and such, I pretended like I was fine. My arm didn't hurt as bad, I was still pretty tired and achy, but this needed to be done. She'd taken care of me and deserved it. We'd been wearing the same clothes for days and days, washing them at night in our sink.

The tension between us was palpable. I grinned as I looked at her feet under the curtain of the changing room. She was trying on some tops she'd found that were frilly and flowy and all those things that girls liked. Yes, the tension was there, and it was more potent than anything I'd ever felt with anyone else. It was like she had a rope tied to me and was yanking for me to come to her. I'd never really experienced sexual tension before...and I loved it.

I already had my jeans, shirts, and a couple pairs of sweatpants to sleep in piled in my arms. So

I was just waiting on Marley and then we'd finally go eat something.

I leaned my good shoulder on the wall next to her room. "You need any help in there?" I let my voice carry the notes of someone who was frustrated, but it had absolutely nothing to do with waiting for her. It was something else entirely.

"I could use some help," I heard behind me. I turned to find a woman peeking out, smirking. "Wanna help me?"

I smiled. "I'm pretty attached to this one here." I jerked my thumb toward Marley's room. "But thanks."

She shrugged with a coy smile and disappeared. When I turned back, Marley was peeking out at me. She had a little smile on her scarred lip that I couldn't figure out. She grabbed my shirt front and pulled me into the room with her. Shutting the curtain, she turned to me and then turned back around, putting her back to me. "I do need some help actually."

There was a half-done zipper on the little blue dress she was wearing. I put my hands on her shoulders, gulping because she was soft in a way that I didn't know women could be. "Up or down?" I asked, but it was a growl if I ever heard one.

Goosebumps ran across her skin then, making me burn in all sorts of ways.

"What?" she breathed. It took me a second to register her shaking.

"The zipper. Up or down."

"Oh," she whispered and took a couple of heaving breaths. "Down. It fits." I didn't move. I didn't dare move yet. "Do you like it?"

"It's a pretty dress," I said evenly, stepping forward a bit.

She turned, letting the zipper-talk go, and looked up at me. "Do girls hit on you everywhere you go?"

"Yes," I answered truthfully. "Girls, women, and even a guy once."

"Your ego must be the size of Lambeau Field."

Holy hell! Did she just make a football joke? "Packers fan, are you?"

"Who isn't?"

Oh, my...gah.... I wiped my face with my palm. "No, my ego isn't the size of a football field because I know they only want to use me. And I used to want to use them, so it didn't matter. I'm the kind of guy that girls want to have a few fun times with, I'm not the settle-down-and-marry kind."

"Why do you say that?" she said incredulously.

"The first woman I was with made sure I knew that." I wasn't bitter about it. It is what is it. I wasn't proud though, and even if Marley left, I'd never be that guy again. "That is a dead life made to trick you into thinking you're living. Girls were the vice and provided the numbness."

She nodded, understanding, but I could tell she didn't really want to know. "I wish I could go back and do things differently."

She smiled sadly and whispered, "Don't we all." I stuck my hands in my pockets, more confused than ever. One minute, I was sure, the next, I was more in the dark than before. What did this girl want from me?

"By the way, that woman was an idiot."

"For hitting on me?" I quirked an amused brow and nodded toward the other changing room.

"No," she laughed. "That, I understand. The woman who told you that you were nothing but a toy...that's not true. I can see you finding that guy that's chasing you, breaking his neck for what he did to your mom, and then you settling down...being a great husband and dad one day."

Dad. That thought had never, ever crossed my mind.

"Really?"

"Yes," she whispered.

"Funny, I see the same about you." I smiled at the picture in my head. "A little girl that looks like you on your hip, all blond hair and pretty cheeks."

She smiled at the floor. "One day," she promised herself. She touched her lip in thought, or self-consciousness.

I lifted her chin until she looked up. I pulled her closer, letting my thumb run down the curve of her nose and stop to rub over that scar. She tried to pull away, but I just held tighter to her cheeks, holding her hostage, trying to give her back a little bit of all the healing she'd given me. She pleaded with me with her eyes, but I refused to release her gaze. The scar was soft and barely made a ridge at all. The pad of my thumb caressed and fell in love with that spot.

"Jude, don't."

"Why?" I said, truly baffled in that moment that she didn't see how I was falling hard for everything about her.

"It's...ugly."

I shook my head, knowing that was going to come out of her mouth. But I understood. I hated my scar, too. And hated when anyone said anything about it. But I... "It's not ugly. I've never wanted to kiss something as much as I want to kiss that scar right now. Gah, Marley, you are absolutely beautiful."

She melted, her body losing it rigidity and her face softening. She pulled one of my hands away so she could reach my jaw. My teeth clamped together. I should have known she'd turn the tables on me. She caressed the scar's length with her thumb as I had done. I stayed still for her ministrations, but wanted to bolt. But when she looked at me, she didn't look at me like it was sexy or like I was some bad boy. She looked at me like she knew exactly how I felt.

That was the only thing that made me stay.

When she leaned forward, pressing her lips to it, I stilled. She reached up on her tiptoes and placed three kisses spread out along it. I waited for it to be over, and begged for it never to be. She leaned back a little and ticked her head to the side. "It's a battle scar, Jude," she said, touching her lip. "Battle scars just remind us that we survived."

I took her face in my hands once more. "We did."

She watched me. "You said you wanted to kiss my scar..." I nodded. "Will you?"

She didn't have to ask me twice.

I lowered onto the sweetest mouth I'd ever tasted and I never wanted to taste another for, God, thank you, she was the only thing that kept me from falling over the edge to the end of me.

I felt her hands bunch in my shirt and that lit my fire. With full pressure and caressing, I gave her everything. She was timid and let me completely lead. I was intrigued, but right then, I wanted to hold the reins. I wanted to show the girl what she had done to me and for me. But later...I wanted to duel.

When I licked at her bottom lip, she gasped in my mouth a little, effectively opening the heavens to me. I was drowning in her taste, living in the air she breathed, swimming in the first moan that escaped her.

The dressing room was small and there were no chairs or benches, just three walls, one mirror, and a curtain. So I couldn't help myself as I turned us and pressed her to the back wall of the dressing room. One of my hands escaped and found its way to her leg. I lifted it to my side, my hand settling in the crook of her knee, feeling how warm and supple she was all over.

Her hand went into my hair, tugging and pulling like a pro. I pressed harder, conveying all the things she was doing to me. Her tongue was timid like she was, but it was nice to feel it brush mine softly, like she was taking her time and savoring me.

Then she reached around and stuck her hand in my back pocket.

I felt my eyes roll to the back of my head under my closed eyelids.

We both jerked when a loud bang resounded through the store. I leaned back, curious. I peeked through the curtain side and my blood ran cold and boiled at the same time.

Biloxi.

Hell.

I looked at her and put my finger over my lips to tell her to be quiet. Her face changed from confused to frightened. I shook my head and whispered in her ear. "It's all right. I'll keep you safe. Do what I say, OK?"

She nodded.

I grabbed Marley's clothes and mine and peeked out once more. He was creating chaos as he badgered the store clerk with a picture. *Two* pictures. He said, "Have you seen these people?"

Dang. He was looking for Marley, too. He wasn't going to let her go. "Come on," I told her and we inched out, her fingers gripping my shirt back. We almost made it to the back door before a shot rang in my ears and the window beside our heads exploded.

Marley screamed and I pulled her in front of me in case the shots weren't finished. People screamed everywhere, yelling, scrambling, running. He'd only made it worse on himself. Now it was harder for him to catch up to us. He was slipping, getting greedy, getting careless. But why?

I pushed her out the door before me and we took off running. We had to ditch the truck, I knew that. I had all our cash that was left on me so we'd be OK if we could just get the heck out of dodge.

We ran across the street just as we heard the alarm go off at the store behind us. Cops would be there soon. At the gas station, an older guy had just filled up and was going in to pay. I grimaced. I hated to do it, but if only he hadn't been trying to pay old school.

I jumped in, throwing the armload in the back. Marley climbed in and scooted to the middle of the bench seat of the old Cutlass. I cranked it up and slammed it into drive. He came out, yelling and cussing, but we were long gone. I flew out onto the highway and looked in my rearview mirror to make sure we were clear.

We weren't.

Biloxi was in my truck and he was closing in. It was a four lane with a light every block or so. I banged my fist on the steering wheel and cursed at my bad luck. Marley turned to look and gasped. She looked at me with wide, begging, innocent eyes, like I had all the answers. "Just keep your head down. It'll be OK," I assured her and hoped I wasn't lying to her.

"Jude...be careful," she said worriedly and kept looking back.

"Just lay down, baby," I heard myself say as I pushed her head down to lay in my lap. She probably thought I was just comforting her, but if he started shooting, I didn't want her hit. She turned sideways as she lay, gripping my leg like a life raft.

I ran the first red light and he followed me. Horns blared and I looked around for a way to lose him. Swerving through traffic that was going thirty-five while I was going fifty and gaining wasn't what I wanted, but that bastard wasn't letting up.

I realized something right then. When we made it out of this situation, I was no longer going to sit back and wait for him to come find me. No. I was going to start looking for him as I promised so long ago.

I looked down at the scared girl who just wanted a normal life. I was going to find out what he wanted with me if it was the last thing I did. I deserved it. She deserved it. It was going to take some shady dealings, but it had to be done.

That murderer was mine.

NINE

A phone rang and I jumped. The old man's phone was in the car, sitting in the empty ashtray. I opened the ancient thing and pressed End Call. Then I got an idea. A genius idea. I told Marley to hold on tight, pressed the button for the camera to come up, and slammed on the brakes.

We flew forward in our seats and in seconds, Biloxi was right next to me out my driver's window. He was so shocked by my maneuver that he didn't even try to fire, but I did. I snapped a picture of his stunned face and then veered off onto a one-way street, going the wrong way, leaving him screeching to a halt and backing up. I was back on the main highway going west instead of east before he made it.

But the big guy was smiling down on us today because a delivery truck pulled right down the one way. There wasn't enough room for them to fit by each other and they both stopped in the middle of the road. I saw him lean out the window, beating his fists on the truck top, before the scene was stolen by a passing building. I relaxed a little and leaned back.

"You can get up. He's gone." She sat up slowly, looking around to affirm my words. "But just to make sure," I said and made a quick turn down the exit for the interstate, "we'll change things up a bit and take the interstate."

"He'll be after us soon, won't he?" she asked, her voice still shaking.

"Yes. He doesn't stop." I didn't look at her for what I said next. "It was the reason I was going to leave you and go on by myself. I didn't want you to be in danger. But he had your picture in there along with mine." I shook my head, wishing I'd been strong enough to do what needed to be done before. "It's too late. He's looking for you, too."

"But wouldn't he assume you'd ditch me?" She turned, her knees in the seat, but she was still next to me. "We didn't know each other. Why would he still be looking for me if he didn't know we were together?"

"I'm not sure, Marley. He's just desperate, I guess."

I sped as fast as I felt safe enough to do without getting pulled over. We only had about two hundred and fifty bucks left, so we had enough for a hotel tonight somewhere. We didn't have enough for a gun, however, and that was next on my list. I'd have to find some work, stat.

We rode in silence, except for the radio. Both our minds were running, I was sure, but I was determined not to let Marley get all scared and worried about this. She sat beside me the entire time, like sitting next to the window would somehow be unsafe. She gripped my arm and let her fingers follow the ridges under my skin to keep herself busy. I knew it was so she wouldn't be taken away by the wave of panic currently settling over her. I felt like a guilty man on death row because all this was my fault. All I could do now was make sure she stayed safe.

After over five hours on the road, I pulled into an old, dilapidated steakhouse with some guy's namesake. "You did promise me steak and yeast rolls."

She smiled at me—the first smile in hours—and reached into the back seat to get one of the pairs of shoes we bought. I hadn't even realized she'd been barefoot the whole time.

I was so exhausted from the day we'd had and driving all afternoon. We hadn't stopped to eat for lunch either. My arm ached a little, but I knew the medicine had done its job and I was going to be fine. They sat us at a booth on the side with a clear view of the stage that was currently being occupied by a large woman belting out some Frank Sinatra's *Fly Me to the Moon*.

We both ordered sweet teas and the waitress brought us a loaf of bread and butter. We dug in. I buttered a piece and put it on her plate for her. She smiled coyly at me. I almost sighed out loud. I figured the fact that she had to know she was in danger because of me was going to be a mood killer. I was glad to see it wasn't.

It was easy for me to shift gears from running to pretending that things were back to normal. I'd done it all my life. But her, she was a rookie at this game, and it surprised me in the best way to see that she didn't fall apart so easily.

"It smells so good in here," she groaned. "I'm going to start eating napkins if they don't bring the food soon."

I laughed. "I'm right there with you." I swallowed my bite and cleared my throat. "I know we're avoiding it, but…I'm sorry about today."

"You mean the shopping spree? Thanks for that." She snapped her fingers. "Rats, we didn't pay!"

"That's not what I mean and you know it," I said softly.

"I know." She scooted over until she was right up against me. I put my arm around her. Her face was so close to mine that I felt her breaths against my cheek. "He's the one with issues, not you. You could have ditched me already and you didn't. I got dumped on you by some weird twist of fate. If you had dropped me off somewhere, he would have me now. You do know that, right?" I let my fingers trail her wrist and it shocked me how satisfied I was when more goosebumps appeared. "You saved me."

I didn't want to hear it. I wanted to wallow and be angry with myself. She pulled my face back up with her cool palm to my cheek. "You don't get to blame yourself."

I sighed and closed my eyes. I let my forehead rest on hers. She was this amazing girl who had dropped into my life, this gift that I didn't know how to accept.

"Thank you."

"Thank you," she rebutted. "For saving my life twice."

One of her feet moved between mine, caressing my ankle and leg as she reached her hand around the back of my neck. *She was playing footsies with me*? I chuckled to myself. No one had ever played footsies with me before.

Instead of over-thinking and being a total girl about this whole 'thing' going on between us, I just lifted her chin and kissed her, because that's exactly what I wanted to do. Her pliable, eager body against mine made it very warm in that restaurant.

It wasn't the frenzied attack it had been at the store. No, this was different. It was an unhurried assault on my senses that I'd never really experienced with someone before. I didn't get enough time to analyze it before the waitress was making shrill noises in her throat to let us know she was there.

She put my plate down. "Aw, are you newlyweds?"

"Uh, no." I laughed, but looked at Marley. "Not quite yet."

I was testing her, seeing if she'd freak. She didn't. Not even a look of shock appeared. Instead, she got this evil little look in her green, sparkling eyes. "No, we're not engaged yet, but my honey here just graduated from college! He's a real, live gynecologist now!"

I choked on my mashed potatoes. She patted me on the back as I took a sip of water. The waitress' eyes widened and she smiled. "Well, congrats. You look a little...young to be a doctor."

"Oh, he worked so hard." Marley's voice had morphed into this cross between a southern bell and cute little hillbilly. "He worked his butt off, he did, and graduated from high school at just sixteen."

"Wow," the waitress said, impressed. "Wow, that's amazing."

"He's a prodigy. My baby." She kissed my cheek, winking and thoroughly enjoying herself.

Alrighty, two can play.

"Well, that's nothing compared to my sugar dumpling here." Marley was barely containing her laughter. She squeezed my thigh under the table. "She won Miss Sweet Corn pageant. That's right, took home the whole shebang, and now we're traveling up for the Miss Watermelon Seed." I looked at her lovingly. "My baby's gonna win and be a star."

"Aw, my goodness! You two are so sweet!" she spouted, clutching her chest.

"Well, thank you."

Marley took a big bite of a roll and spoke with her mouth full. "You wouldn't happen to have a *Congratulations, I'm a doctor now* cake back there, would you?"

"Um..." she looked around. "No. Sorry."

"That's OK!" she waved her fork at her. "Don't you worry about it."

"Well, congratulations to you both. I hope you enjoy your dinner. Everything all right so far?"

"Oh, it's delish," Marley answered through her food.

The waitress nodded and left with a smile. The woman on stage crooned some old love song as Marley and I laughed into each other's shoulders. She gripped my thigh under the table and I gripped hers.

"You're hilarious," I told her and cut into my steak. It wasn't the best in the world, but it was food and it was hot and not in a can. It was heaven.

"*You're* funny," she said, her eyes on her plate. I looked over because her voice seemed different. She was staring at her steak, and then her eyes moved over to her knife.

I got it.

"You want me to cut it up for you?"

She took a deep breath. "I haven't had steak in years. Since I was like...five or something."

I squeezed my fingers on her thigh. "Is that why you wanted to eat steak today?"

"Partly. I knew I'd have to use silverware to eat it." She sighed. "I know that's so stupid, that I don't use forks, but..." She shrugged. "When I was five...or something...we were eating steak. Foster home number four. I was cutting my steak, a little too loudly, and they got mad. I was so scared they were going to send me away that I started shaking and dropped my fork to the floor. The mom threw an entire stack of forks from the drawer on the floor in her fit."

My jaw clenched, my fist tightening. She just kept breaking my heart with her stories.

"She didn't allow me to eat with utensils after that and so...I just never did. Because I was scared when I was a kid of dropping it and when I got older, I never knew what or where I'd be eating. I just...never."

She picked up her knife and looked at it like it was alien. Her fork was next and she started to cut into her steak. She took a bite from the fork and then got a bite of mashed potatoes next. She licked the fork clean and laughed before looking over at me.

I was absolutely enthralled. It wasn't that she didn't know how to use a fork, it was that she'd been scared into thinking she wasn't worthy of one. I couldn't look away. We'd both broken down so many barriers since we'd met and there she was, breaking another one, and letting me be a part of it all with her.

When dessert came, we shared one piece of cheesecake slowly. I watched as she licked her fork over and over again.

"What now? Hotel or road?"

"I'm beat," I answered truthfully. "I just want to sleep and then we can hit the road in the morning."

"Sounds good."

She took the last bite and had a little bit on the edge of her lip. I shook my head. Another cliché scenario, but I was *so* going for it.

I leaned in close. She saw what was coming and her lips parted. "You've got a little bit right here." I licked it off before going in and taking her entire mouth with mine. She dropped her fork loudly to the table with a clank, but she didn't seem worried about it being thrown back at her. She devoured me as I devoured her.

The waitress again got our attention and I paid her cash, telling her to keep the change. We rushed out together, both of us eager to get somewhere alone, somewhere private. "Good luck in the pageant!" the waitress yelled.

"Thank you!" Marley yelled back.

She giggled on the way to the car. We drove the two blocks to the motel and got a room. I took her hand as we walked up the stairs. She was rubbing my arm and pressing against my side. I pulled my arm around her, getting as close as I could. We reached the room and she leaned her back against the wall beside the door. I followed her to keep the contact. I fidgeted with the key, but she couldn't wait and pulled me down roughly to kiss her.

The male in me was awakened.

We pulled and tugged on each other as I tried to get the key in without looking. Her tongue wasn't tame and timid like before. No, she was wild and on fire as much as I was. Finally, I cursed against her mouth and leaned back to get the door unlocked. As soon as I did, I threw it open while pulling her in with me, kissing all the while. I slammed and locked the door impressively without looking and then turned to press her to the wall.

She was panting and warm all over. I ran my hand up her leg, pushing her dress up a little on the outside of her thigh. She tugged my shirt until I lifted my arms and it was tossed away. I'd never been this turned on in my life. Ever. I was about to implode with the want to have her.

She lifted that one leg I was caressing and hooked it around my hip. Her arms were around my neck and our lips attacked and fought each other. When she moaned softly, I was done.

I hoisted her up, ignoring the pull in my shoulder, and placed both of her legs around my waist, kissing her harder. When I let my hand ride up her ribs to the soft place I wanted, she gasped. It made me pause. She was excited, yes, but this was different.

All the little clues and pieces started to fit together. Today, her kiss being so timid. She said she'd never had a hickie. She'd been in and out of foster homes. Changing schools. She didn't even have a place to live... Oh, gah...

"You've never done this, have you?" I asked through a ragged breath. She stayed quiet. "I mean, after what happened to you..."

She huffed. "Why are you asking me that?"

"Uh..." I looked between us. "I think it's a valid question for the girl I have pressed to the wall."

She sighed. "No, but it doesn't matter. I don't want to stop."

She kissed the corner of my mouth and pulled me closer. I shook my head at myself. *Don't do it...don't be the good guy here...she's ready, she wants you...*

Daggum it.

"I can't." The look of hurt and disappointment was expected. I rushed to explain. "I don't want your first time to be like this."

"So you'll sleep with those other girls, but not me?" She hadn't said it facetiously, it was a genuine inquiry. Again, I hated myself and my past.

"I'm going to be honest. I always want to be honest with you." She nodded. "I had sex with those girls because I used them to be a distraction from my crappy life. They didn't mean anything, and I know that sounds bad, but I didn't mean anything to them either." Kate flitted through my mind and I felt guilty all over again. "I don't want anything in our past to define...what you and I will be."

She paused to think that over. "Why do we have to wait? We're both here. We're alone. I won't hold anything in your past against you. I promise. And if you're worried about my past, what happened to me, don't. The whole situation was different. It's light in here, I can see you. I won't freak out. I know it's you."

"It's not that, sweetheart. I just..." So much for not sounding like a chick. "I don't want your first time to be in a hotel."

"But it's not my first time," she said softly, looking at my neck instead of my eyes.

I made her look up at me. "Oh, yes it is. You *give* your first time to the one you want to be with. That can't be taken from you." She smiled, tears lining her lashes. "I don't want to have sex, Marley, I want to make love to you." She sighed, putting her forehead to mine. "I've never made love to a girl before. I want to, with you, but not while we're on the run from some guy who's made it his life's work to kill me. This hotel, where other people have slept and cheated on their spouses and... I want us to have a clean slate. I don't want your first time to be tainted by all this. I don't want *our first time* to be tainted by all this. You don't deserve to be taken in a rush, you deserve to be worshiped."

She watched my face with a look of awe. She looked like she might cry again. I didn't want that.

"I'm sorry. I'm not trying to hurt your feelings. I want you. I want you...so bad. I just need to do what's right by you."

She laughed softly. "You have been. I thought I'd be scared." She smiled, but she was crying again. "I thought the memory of what happened to me would rule and ruin everything when I finally did want to be with someone...but you took all that away." She took my face in her hands. "I feel safe with you, completely, and I know when you finally...make love to me, I won't have any dirt left, nothing left to feel filthy about, nothing left to distract me from the real world and real life. It's only been a little more than a week, but you make everything better."

I didn't know what to say. I wanted to boo-hoo a little myself if she kept that up. But I felt the same way about her. I was falling so hard for this girl. She made everything clean. "Will you at least kiss me?" She smiled. "Is that acceptable?"

"More than," I answered, but wondered... "Have you ever made out with someone before?"

"I've only kissed one guy before you, and it was in his backyard on a squeaky swing. It wasn't that great," she admitted, adoringly sheepish.

"Well," I replied, moving her hand from my bare chest and wrapping it around the back of my neck. "Challenge accepted, sweetheart."

I teased. It was so mean, I knew that, but it was so fun to watch her, everything new to her eyes, as I inched my mouth to hers with an entirely new purpose in mind. I still planned to pin her to the panel walls, but not for sex. As I sank into her mouth and felt the warmth run through my veins, I realized it had been forever since I'd just made out with a girl, since I had foreplay and a reason to make a girl sigh other than the inevitable end result. I grinned into our kiss as I felt the first of many rays of sunshine beam right into my soul. This was more than fun, it was therapy. She was healing me one touch at a time and didn't even know it.

I kissed her with everything in me, all that I was and had to offer. I unleashed it all on her and didn't apologize. I wanted to consume her...because she was consuming me.

TEN

To keep the mood PG, I placed her feet back to the floor, but kept her right there for what seemed like hours. I was able to shave this time, but my five o'clock was coming in, I was sure. It seemed wrong to make her pretty white skin pink with my rubbing, but I was in too deep to stop.

She never once grabbed my bad shoulder. She remembered and, though her hands and fingers roamed me, they never hit the bad spot. Another sign of how thoughtful and awesome she was.

Eventually, I moved us to the bed and though Neanderthalish, I had one task in mind when I finally let her lips go and moved south to her neck and then her collarbone and then the spot behind her ear. That's when I heard it. The gasp that meant they'd never experienced anything like it and their bodies undulate without their permission at the feel of it. I grinned to myself at finding treasure and stayed at that spot, pressing in closer to her, freaking loving the way her hands gripped my head and she breathed into my hair as if I was the only thing keeping her from falling over the cliff edge.

But she didn't know yet, that was exactly what I planned to do one day.

For hours, I kissed her into oblivion. After we'd had our fill, I put her under the covers with me, enjoying the feel of just sleeping next to someone.

The next morning, I woke first and just watched her for a minute. Her blond hair was lying over half her face and she was still curled right up against me. She looked so peaceful, like she knew she was safe with me. I had to find Biloxi and end this. I couldn't let her down.

I leaned over her and kissed her nose. "Get up, beautiful."

She scrunched her face and pushed at my chest. "Shut up."

I laughed and swooped down for another wake-up kiss to her cheek. "Get up, gorgeous."

She groaned. I kissed her eyelid. "Get up, sweet face."

She giggled into my shoulder. "Oh, my gosh, stop. Please. One more nickname and I'll hit you."

"They're not nicknames, they're adjectives. Get up. We've got errands to run."

She looked at me curiously, pushing her hair back. "What kind of errands? Job hunting?"

"That, too. But first, some breakfast and a library."

She smirked. "Taking up a new hobby?"

"Nope, just playing detective." I pulled the old man's phone from my pocket. It was almost dead. Hopefully, he had a charger in the car. I opened the camera and showed her. "I got the bastard's face and Google image search is hopefully going to help tell me about him."

"From a runaway to a tech geek. Wow."

"You laugh," I tickled her until she was hitting me to stop, "but I've got skills."

"OK, OK, OK!" She laughed and palmed my cheek. "You gonna shave first?"

I squinted. "Did I hurt you last night?" I rubbed my stubbled jaw. "I thought it-"

"Of course you didn't hurt me last night." She sighed and her eyes shined with something I couldn't process. I fell into her deep eyes and willingly let her keep me prisoner. I knew we were now talking about more than beard burn. "Thank you...for last night."

I braced my arm on the bed by her head. "I should be thanking you."

"Because I begged for it? Is that why? Is there some innate, primal thing in a male that likes it when a woman begs?"

I chuckled and shook my head a 'no', but said, "Yes."

She sighed exasperatingly and turned her face away in jest. "I knew it. Another one bites the dust."

I laughed harder. "You're funny," I told her again. "Maybe we can get you a job in stand-up."

"I'm only funny to you, I'm afraid."

"That waitress last night thought you were funny," I countered and leaned forward to run my nose down her jaw. "A gynecologist was the best you could come up with?"

"No, but it was the funniest thing I could come up with."

I started to chuckle, but came across the hickie I'd given her last night, right under her ear. A split second of worry that she'd be upset ran across my mind before my ego took over and I was smiling smugly against her skin.

"What are you smiling about?"

"Nothing," I lied and leaned up to kiss her. She kissed back, once again content to let me take her for a ride wherever I was going. "What a beautiful mess we're in," I murmured.

She smiled at that. "And what does that mean?" she whispered.

"I think you know."

She bit her lip and nodded. "It's a sucky situation, but…there's you."

"And there's you," I countered and kissed her again. I sighed and leaned back a little. "I'm buying a gun today." She stilled. "Not just to keep you safe, but to find him. I can't live on the edge of the knife anymore, Marley. I can't just wait for him to come find me and hope I can get away. I need to find him and make sure that he never finds you."

She didn't say anything, but she looked at me. "I used to be in the gun club. We went to the range every week."

"To be honest, I was surprised you didn't have one already. What do you do to defend yourself when he shows up?"

I twisted my lips. "I run. It's what my mom made me promise to do. But it's different now."

She nodded. "Let's get going."

I ran down and got our clothes out of the car. We put some of the new ones on and headed out. I watched her from behind, her heels flipping over her flip-flops. Her boots were gone, abandoned at the store we had to flee. I bet she missed them. I know I did.

I told her we needed to ditch the car as we rode down the main strip of town. We'd take a bus or something to the next city, help cover our trail by not keeping the same vehicle. I should have dumped my truck before I did.

So, I pulled into the back of a lot and left it there. I took the phone charger and left everything else behind.

"Breakfast," I said in a flourish, opening the door to the diner. We ate on the same side of the booth this time and every time her elbow rubbed mine, I found myself looking over at her. Somehow, she was already looking at me. She giggled every time and then went back to eating, our legs touching.

We walked to the library, that the waitress said was only six blocks away, thankfully. We started out on the sidewalk and she took my hand in hers.

I looked down at them intertwined and felt another ray of sunshine break through. I'd never held hands with anyone before.

"Is this OK?" she asked, curious of my reaction.

I stopped on the sidewalk, keeping her hand in mine, and kissed her right there. She tasted like the orange juice she'd just had. I pulled her stunned figure with me as we moved along and the library came into view. It was one of those old colonial, southern ones.

We looked both ways and crossed the two-lane. We got to use the computers for one hour only and then we'd have to come back the next day to use it again, so we needed to go fast.

I put Marley in a chair and pulled one up beside her by the computer. I took the USB end of his charger and plugged it in, transferring the picture to the computer desktop. I held my breath as I dropped the image into the search engine.

Marley and I both caught our breath at what we saw. His name would always be Biloxi to me, but his real name was Vincent DoMaggio. He'd been indicted for several things, but the company he worked for had been in trouble as well. The company's name—BioGene, Inc.

My heart felt sluggish in my chest as I realized what kind of products a company named that would produce.

But the thing that caught our eye was a picture next to Biloxi's. Our friendly neighborhood hotel rescuer. She looked at me, but pointed at him. "How…Why? If he had us, right there, why didn't he snatch us up then?"

"I don't know," I answered truthfully. "I don't understand any of this."

So I started printing. Page after page of anything that looked important, pictures, and business addresses spit out of the printer. By the time we were done, our hour was up and the ten cents a page bill we racked up was twelve dollars and thirty cents.

We took our stack of papers and went back to the hotel to go through it all.

"Look here," she said. "Look at this."

Her voice had taken on a shaky tone since we'd found the picture of the guy who had helped her. She'd been so close and could have been taken then. That would have been it.

I went and sat on the bed behind her, putting my knee on her other side, and leaned her back into my frame. I hated that she was involved in this now. I scanned the page she showed me. It was talking about genetics testing, cancer scan levels, fatalities of newborns and fetuses, a list of drugs and what they did to each subject…test subjects…

Test subjects?

My fingers instinctively went to the port scar near my ribs. I stood and ran my hand through my hair. "What did she do?" I asked. Had my mom willingly signed up for something to be done to her?

"What?" she asked. "Do you remember something?"

"No, but…" I pulled up my shirt and showed her the IV port I'd had since I was a baby. "Mom told me this was for IVs when I was a baby. She would never tell me why, just said *they* gave it to me."

She was visibly trembling. "Marley?" I knelt down in front of her. "Marley, what is it, baby?"

"I hadn't noticed your scar before." She looked in my eyes as her trembling hand reached for her shirt hem. I knew it before she showed me, but I still begged for it not to be so, because that meant that there was way more to the story than just some guy with a grudge hunting me down. She lifted the hem and showed me the scar from the port.

The scar that looked exactly like mine.

That afternoon, we put all the stuff away and went to the nearest pawn shop. He said we had to wait three days for the paperwork to go through. I sagged on the glass in disappointment. No paperwork. I hadn't thought of all that. When I asked him if there was any way to cut through the red tape, he told us to get out.

So we went to look for some work instead. We needed, now more than ever, to find out the whos and whats and whys behind all this. The address for

BioGene's headquarters said New Mexico and that was exactly where I was going.

Where *we* were going.

Marley had made it perfectly clear by her glare that she had every intention of seeing this out with me and for whatever reason, we found each other in the dark that night on the bend when we collided. I told her I'd tell the police, get her put somewhere safe until I could come back after everything was taken care of. She wouldn't hear of it and stayed angry all through lunch for even suggesting it.

Now, as we walked hand-in-hand in our unintentionally matching black Chuck Taylor's down Main Street, looking for a quick buck, I was speechless at how much I was falling for her. Even with all the crap raining on us, she didn't let it haunt her, didn't let it sour her. Just like her past, she was above it.

"Maybe they did some kinda tests on us and we can never get sick?" she said and ticked her head to look at me. "Or maybe we'll have spidey sense."

I smiled. "I doubt it's anything that cool."

It started to rain, but Marley didn't seem to mind, so neither did I. I could see a farm on the edge of town, the cornfields brown and dead, but I still took us down the dirt driveway. There had to be something we could do there.

The farmer was in the barn and saw us coming. We were both soaked. He wiped grease off his hands and tipped his head. "Afternoon."

"Afternoon, sir."

He laughed. "Oh, boy. When young folks start off with manners, you know they're about to ask you for something."

That almost threw off my game, but I forged on. "No, sir." He grinned at that. "We were just wondering if you had some work you needed done around here. We're passing through and haven't had the best of luck. Just…if there's anything you can think of, anything, we'll do it."

He looked between us. "Sorry. Got nothing."

He turned to go. "Sir, please."

"I ain't about to supply two runaways with drug money. Now, get off my property."

"We're not drug addicts and we're not runaways," Marley told him. He turned to look at her. She released my hand and stepped toward him, just one step. "We're orphans. We both go to college," she pulled her student ID from her back pocket, "see and we're really hard workers. We're just trying to find out some things about our birth parents and have had car trouble and…all sorts of things."

He sighed, too long and too meaningful. He didn't believe her. "Come on, Marley." I took her arm. "He doesn't believe you. Let's go."

She gripped my arm as we turned and left. We'd find something else. We had to soon enough because the money would run out. It always did.

He called to us, "Hey!" I turned my head back, but Marley faced away. "I need the field shoveled, the chicken coop painted, and the stumps out by the pond pulled up. I'll give you exactly four hundred dollars to do it all and not a penny more."

I nodded. He started to walk back to the barn. He turned and raised his salt and pepper eyebrow. "You just gonna stand there or follow me and get to work?"

"I've done worse," Marley assured me as we shoveled cow dung into a wheelbarrow. "I used to work at that bar, remember? Nothing better than getting slapped on the behind by a guy that just puked on the floor that you now have to clean."

I growled under my breath. "Don't talk about that place. Even then, I hated the idea of you working there."

She straightened and adjusted the bandana over her nose. "Aw. Are you jealous?"

I flung the poo harder. "Hell no." Then I looked at her and grinned. "Hell yes."

She laughed. "Don't hit on me when we're shoveling crap, Jude!"

When it was full, we went and dumped it in the garden to be tilled and then went back for more. We were done with task number one in a few hours and started in on the chicken coop, but darkness came and so did my hunger. We told him we'd be back the next day to finish up and he said, "You're dang right you will, 'cause you're not getting paid 'til you do."

We got cheap tacos from this little stand by the farmer's market and stopped to eat them at the outside tables. The street was loud, but it was good to sit among people, listen to them talk and laugh around us. I watched Marley watch a couple as they bounced a baby back and forth, the baby laughing and giggling.

I could hold it in no longer. "Are we gonna talk about it?"

"May as well," she said softly, her eyes never leaving the baby—the baby that reminded us both of what we'd seen on those papers in our hotel. She looked at me, her eyes hard. "He's not just after you, now he's after me, too. At least I know you're not going to dump me off somewhere now to save me, right?"

Ouch.

She squeezed her eyes closed for a few seconds and then looked right into mine. "I'm sorry. That wasn't fair. I know you were just trying to protect me."

I sighed, pushing my taco trash aside, and took her hand in both of mine. "I thought I was cursed."

Her brow dipped to a 'v'. "What?"

"My mom tried to protect me and…" I shrugged. "It was my fault that she died."

She squeezed my fingers. "Please, please don't tell me we're playing the blame game. You *know*. You have to know that it wasn't your fault. She was your mom!" she shrieked, worked up in my defense. She calmed and spoke quieter. "Would you rather have a mom that just flat didn't care about you?"

I noticed the nerve that was hit in her voice. I gave her a questioning look to tell her to go on. "My mom didn't die—she left me. She brought me to the hospital when I was three and said she didn't want me. That began my parade through every foster home in the state that hated children."

She was shaking and I hated that. I scooted over on the bench and rubbed my hand on the small of her back, circles and squares and odd shapes.

Anything to soothe her. She went on. "So, when I hear you say how little you value the way your mom cared for you?" She shook her head violently. "Nuhuh. Nuhuh, Jude."

"I valued her. I loved her so much it completely broke me when she died," I explained. "She was the only person in my life and then I was all alone, fending for myself, stealing, anything to survive. I hate that she *had* to die for me. I'm not saying I don't appreciate it."

"It wasn't your fault. You're going to get your justice on them, Jude. We both are. And then we'll finally be able to move on."

I had a thought. "And I wonder about your mom, too." She gave me a look. "No, listen. Did you go into the system as a Jane Doe or did she give them your birth certificate?"

"The state named me. I didn't have anything with me."

"See," I said with renewed vigor, "I bet she did for you what I was trying to do. Get you away from me for your own good. If you were not with me, then when they found me, you wouldn't be harmed. I bet she thought the same thing. I bet she thought if she put you in the system as a Jane Doe they'd bounce you around and Biloxi would never find you."

A spark of real hope and gratefulness shown through. "You really think so? Maybe?"

"It makes sense." I cupped her cheek. "No one would throw you away."

She smiled, but it was the ugly-cry, happy kind. The release kind. I pulled her to me and rubbed her arm as I hugged her and waited for her to let it all go. "You're getting really good at this."

I smirked. "At what?"

"Being human." She lifted her head. "Thank you. I'm…so glad you're here."

I huffed a happy breath and let my fingers caress her cheek slowly with the tips, accepting the sunshine that blasted through me. She closed her eyes, soaking in my touch. When we were both about to fall asleep and the bugs were flying around the street lamps, we threw our stuff away and headed out.

But we didn't go to the hotel like she thought. I pulled her into the drugstore, right to the shampoo aisle, and stopped in front of the hair dyes. She looked at me, missing the point. I waited—I knew she'd get it.

When she did, it was one of the saddest things ever. "No, not my hair, Jude!" she whined.

"We have to. Both of us. It'll help, especially since we know there's more than one of these guys.

He was right under our nose and we didn't even know it."

She pouted and looked them over. Her lips pulled to the side and she picked up a box that was just a shade darker blond than she was now. I smiled sadly. "Nice try."

She rolled her eyes and searched again before grabbing a chestnut brown. I only knew it was chestnut because it was stated boldly on the box. I grabbed black and a pair of cheap clippers. We paid and when we got to the hotel, she went first. I knew she was just getting it over with. She stayed in there the entire time and I waited, with only football to keep me company. The Jags were smoking the Titans when I heard the hair dryer start.

Ten minutes later, the door opened to a dark-haired beauty. Holy...she was a bombshell. The dark hair made her skin look like porcelain and her lips looked red and plump even with no make-up on.

"Your silence speaks volumes," she muttered wryly and started to close the door.

I jumped up and stopped her, groaning a little when my shoulder hit the doorframe, and pushed her to the wall to keep her there. I didn't waste any time on pretenses. "My God in heaven, Marley...you are breathtaking."

She sighed. I kept going. "I'm totally serious. Marley, baby, you look…incredible. You're a bombshell like this."

"It doesn't matter anyway. I had to do it to keep them from noticing me so easily, not for looks," she sulked.

"And wow, you are so adorable with your lip poked out like that."

She laughed. "Ok, you can stop now."

I smiled and touched her neck where the mark I'd given her still was.

"I owe you one, by the way," she muttered and leaned up to kiss me, too quickly.

"Owe me what?" My lips twisted into a smirk. "I've got to tell you, I like the sound of that."

She grinned. "Owe you one of these," she explained, leaning her neck to the side while holding her collar away. I pursed my lips, full on accepting the guilt. She then leaned up again and kissed the exact spot behind my ear. I made an embarrassing noise in my throat, but she pulled back, again, too quickly.

"Maybe later," she quipped, winking before she turned.

"*Come on*," I complained, half playing, half *so* not playing.

She giggled at my misery. "Hurry up. I can't wait to see what *the new you* looks like."

I smiled. "It looks just like this."

She bit her lip, understanding, and nodded as she shut the door.

ELEVEN

When I came out, she was on the bed's edge, looking over the papers strewn out everywhere to see them better. Not only had I dyed my hair black, but I'd taken the clippers with the size two attached and took almost all of it off. Her mouth opened soundlessly.

I ran my hand along my head. "It's short."

"You look like a marine."

But she hadn't just said it, she *breathed* it. I quirked an amused brow. "Is that right?" She swallowed and nodded. "Let me guess—you've got a thing for marines?"

She shook her head and threw a shirt at me from the pile, laughing. "Shut up."

I sat opposite her and started looking around all the papers. "Find anything?"

"The thing is that I don't even know what I'm looking for. I could be looking at something really important right in the face and not see it for what it is."

She scattered them around in a frenzy and laughed. "All these wasted trees. You know…" She stopped for a long time, collecting herself. I waited and watched as the emotions played over her face. The light from the lamp in the corner was dim, only lighting half of her face. Finally she spoke again, smiling softly. "I don't have many memories of my mom at all. I was only three when she left me, but there's this one memory of us. We were sitting under this big willow tree. It was massive, or maybe it just looked that way because I was so small. I don't remember what we talked about or anything, I just remember lying under it, watching the branches above us. It felt like something we did all the time. Willow trees have always been my favorite because of that. Even though she left me, I just can't let go of that tree."

She looked up at me, strangely shy. "Is that silly?"

"Of course not. And we're going to prove that you're mom didn't dump you because she didn't want you. I just know it."

"Please," I heard her whisper as she started looking at papers again.

I turned some of the papers to face me, with renewed vigor. I found BioGene's company financials, since they obviously were a publicly traded company, all the names of their CEOs and head this and head that. Then all the info on their not-for-profit side. The scientific research side.

It was supposed to sound so on the up-and-up, which made it sound so shady.

We read over everything for hours, changing positions, her lying on the bed, me in the chair, her Indian style on the floor, me leaning on the back wall. My shoulder was aching from all the stretching from dyeing my hair. I rolled my shoulders and focused in on the paper again.

It was all these random names and dates. They were labeled "Project 23". But there were more than twenty-three names and the dates didn't match that either, so it must have been some name they chose for whatever this was. There were pages of them as I counted along…and then there she was. My mom.

I had expected it, knew it, but it still hammered into my chest at seeing it.

Veronica Mae Jackson - December 19, 1991

My freaking birthday.

I looked up at Marley as she leaned her head back against the bed and yawned. "You don't know anything about your mom? You don't know your real name?"

She shook her head. "No, nothing. Why?"

"I just found my mom's name on this paper."

She gasped and bolted up to my side. "Oh, my gosh! What? What does it say?" She scanned the list to where I was pointing.

"Just a date. My birthday."

She looked up at me, as if to say, 'Are you OK?' I nodded and then told her what I knew to be true. "Your mom's on this list somewhere. One of these names is your mom."

She didn't look at the list, she looked up at me. I waited for her to be ready. I whispered, "Do you know your birthday? When is it?"

"If feels so strange," she told me, gripping my arm, "being this close to her, but still being so far away." She was debating whether she even wanted to know.

I leaned down and kissed her. It was becoming so easy to be this guy. The guy who cherished one thing above all else and wasn't just filled with hate. It was surprisingly easy to fall in love with this girl after a lifetime of wanting anything but. I blamed her.

I blamed her in the best way.

She leaned back just enough to breathe. She licked her lips, her tongue touching my lip with the movement, and whispered. "I knew my birthday and I knew my first name. They just gave me a last name to go with it." I nodded. "January 31st, 1995."

I found it pretty quickly on the next page below my mom's. It was then I realized that the birthdays went in order. Each month had one birth and the next month, another baby was born. I met her eyes again.

"Elizabeth Violet Sanford," I told her and watched her face crumple as she received the first puzzle piece of where she came from.

I let the paper float to the floor and pulled her to me, rocking her in my arms as she cried for the life she missed out on.

It was late at that point, so I picked her up and took her to the bed with me. I held onto her the entire time and put her on my lap as I settled against the headboard. She had helped me work through so much crap and it felt amazing to be able to return the favor.

Eventually, after several tissues and over an hour later, she took the remote from the nightstand and turned on some old episode of Seinfeld. When she laughed at the Soup Nazi, I knew the crisis was over. I felt my whole body relax. We fell asleep watching old episodes and finally, after all this time, had pieces of ourselves put back into place.

Now, we just had to go to this place and find out what exactly they had done to our mothers.

And to us.

"Put your back into it, boy!" he yelled.

I turned to the farmer and gave him a look. "Sir, we get paid the same amount, no matter how much time it takes us, right? So, please...I've got it under control."

Truth was, my shoulder was killing me to the point of crying like a freaking sissy. But I wasn't about to cop out. We needed the money, plus Marley would just try to pick up my slack and I couldn't have that.

He had evil eyed us when we came up with our dark hair. "Knew it," he said under his breath and then smiled condescendingly. "All right, runaways, let's get to work."

Ever since then, he'd been on our butts to get the job finished and get gone. We had two stumps left. It was after three in the afternoon, the sun was hot and pissed off, and I was so ready to be done. My shoulders were burned, I could tell. I had to ditch my shirt when the stump grinding came up. Throwing that ax over my shoulder and thumping it into the wood was back breaking work, but I was used to the labor. Marley tried to keep up, picking up all the stray twigs and slivers and putting them in the tinderbox, but it had been an awfully long, hot day.

I watched him as he walked away, heading to the chicken coop to check out the work we'd finished up there today. I threw my ax into one of the logs and told Marley to stay there. I ran to his barn and laughed when the keys were right there in the ignition of the John Deere. I looked until I found a chain thick enough and tossed it on before cranking it up.

I used to drive one of those every day when I was in high school. I worked on a woman's farm and she let me live in the loft of the barn where they stored all the junk they couldn't bear to part with. So I knew all the ins and outs of a farm. And the old man may have wanted us to hack for four days at those stumps with an ax, but it wasn't happening.

I drove the tractor out of the barn, careful not to clip the door with the hookup, and he turned to look at me, hands on his hips. I tipped an imaginary hat to him. He shook his head, but I saw the small smile. He waved his hands at me in an *I give up* manner before turning back to his task.

When I reached the stump, I took it out of gear and hopped down to attach the chain around it before I hopped back on. I held my hand out and yelled, "Would the lady like a ride?"

She giggled. I saw it, but couldn't hear it. Pity. "Love to, stud!" she yelled back. I hoisted her up to sit on my knee.

Her tank top showed her sunburn as well. I kissed the side of her neck, *my spot*, before putting the tractor in gear and letting it buck and pull, before giving it slack and going at it again. Marley held on tight for the ride and when the stump finally gave way, pulling the roots out and tipping it up on its side, she squealed, "This is so much fun!"

I laughed and we repeated the process for the next stump, which was a little more stubborn than the first. After that, I went and pulled the wood splitter over. It took us a couple hours to split it all and stack it between the trees he told us to. I parked the tractor and put my shirt back on, exhausted. I didn't even want to eat, just get in bed.

He met us half way as we walked toward his house. He had the cash in his hand and folded it in half, giving it all to me. I stuck it in my pocket and told him thanks and we appreciated it. He nodded, but then said, "Can I talk to you for a minute, son?"

I looked at Marley and back to him. "Uh, sure." As we walked a few feet away, I told him, "By the way, my name's Jude. We never properly introduced ourselves."

"Myron." He shook my hand and looked over at Marley as he spoke. "She was telling the truth, wasn't she? You're not runaways."

"No, sir. We're not."

"I didn't think you'd come back today after I didn't pay you yesterday, but you did come back and you're not an idiot. You know how to do things and you both work hard... You're too young to be such hard workers unless you been doing it all your life."

I stayed quiet. I didn't think he was looking for an answer.

"You've been walking here every day. You don't have a car so how are y'all leaving town?"

"We'll probably take the bus."

"Where you headed?"

"New Mexico."

"What's in New Mexico?" he asked. Nosy old man.

"Answers," I said and looked over at Marley. "And hopefully, a way of life where looking over our shoulder isn't a requirement."

He smiled. "You're in love with that little girl."

I should have balked, I should have laughed... "Yes, sir, I sure am."

"Is it the law you're in trouble with?" he asked, his head cocked toward the barn.

I shook my head. "It's...someone who's got a grudge on our parents. But they're long gone."

He sighed and then nodded his head for me to follow him. I beckoned Marley to me and followed him to the big, white barn. She took my hand and whispered, "Is everything OK?"

I nodded. When I looked back at him, he was pulling the tarp off an old Chevy pick-up truck. It was beautiful. He had restored the black paint and glass. I wondered why he was showing it to us.

"It's been kept up for a while, but I take her out and run her about once a month just to make sure she's good to go. She was a project truck. My wife hated this vehicle with her very being because I spent so much time and money on it, but when it was all finished, she always wanted to take this when we went to town. I know if she were here, she'd give you some supper and homemade bread to take with you...but she's not here and I can't cook to barely keep my own self alive, let alone two other folks."

I waved him off. "It's fine. We appreciate the help. I'm sorry about your wife." Marley gripped my hand tighter.

"Me, too," he said with sad, far away smile. "This is the only way I can help you," he told me, holding out the keys. The keychain was an old

Texaco logo. I looked up at him like he was an insane person. "Take it. I ain't pulling your leg."

"No," I said, surprising myself with the force of it. "Sir...I don't deserve it."

Marley's face was full of sympathy as she rubbed her hand across my chest. "Jude."

"I've made too many mistakes," I explained. "I've done...so many things I'm not proud of to survive."

"So become a politician," he joked and gripped my shoulder. It burned under his palm from the sunburn. "Take the truck, son. When you're a starving man and you're offered a loaf of bread, you take it."

I hesitated in my guilt at what I'd done. Marley squeezed my hand again and I looked over at her. I would steal as many cars, do as many odd jobs, and hurt as many bastards that it took to keep her safe.

I didn't know what happened, but she was mine. However it happened...she was mine now.

I looked back at Myron. "Thank you."

"No need-ooph..." Marley slammed into him with a hard hug. He laughed and hugged her back. I smiled at her and took the keys he held out once more.

"Really, thank you," she said and beamed up at him.

Marley climbed into the truck and looked over all the white leather.

"Just take care of her," he told me and shook my hand for the last time.

"Don't worry," I assured him. "I won't take her over sixty-five."

He laughed. "Wasn't talking 'bout the truck, son."

I huffed a laugh. "I will."

I hopped in and we drove through a drive-thru before heading back to the hotel. We ate and crashed big time.

The next morning, we both moaned and groaned about our sunburns as we got dressed and packed everything up to check out. With all our clothes and the papers in one trash bag, we loaded up. We hit the road for breakfast before leaving town and headed west.

We started to pull into the diner we'd eaten at that day, but I slammed on the brakes when we saw the car we abandoned in the back of the lot being torn apart by several burly men. I looked for Biloxi and didn't see him, so I figured it was just the cops. I started to breathe a sigh when his head popped up from behind the open door. He was red in the face with anger, but hadn't seen us.

I put us in reverse and pulled back onto the highway. "Well, looks like no breakfast," I told her as we sped as fast as limits would allow on the way out of town.

"How does he keep finding us?"

"I don't know," I told her truthfully. "But I'm done with him for now. My main goal is to get to that facility and see what was going on when our moms were there. Then, he's mine."

She nodded. "I agree."

"You know what? You still got your cell?" I pulled the old man's cell I had from my pocket and tossed it out the window. I saw it smash on the road in the rear view mirror.

She shook her head. "I left it behind. It died a long time ago anyway."

She leaned back, putting her knees up on the dash, turned on the radio, and rested her head on my shoulder. I let my hand rest on the inside of her thigh, shifting gears between her knees when I needed to, and focused on getting us as far away from him as possible.

TWELVE

We only stopped for gas and food for the next sixteen hours. I drove, then she drove, then I drove, and then she slept with her head in my lap. Finally, I could take no more and checked into another crummy hotel.

The next morning we were on the road again, another state, another day of travel. And we talked a lot, which was a new concept for me. She told me about how many schools she'd been to and how many of her foster moms made her call them 'Mother'. Gross.

I told her about the schools I'd been to and how I'd never gotten to play football or sports. How I spent too much time with silly girls and goofing off instead of focusing on school like I should of. She kinda tensed at that and it made me pause. "What's up?"

"Nothing," she lied so badly.

What the hell? "Tell me."

She turned, putting her back to the truck door and her feet in my lap. "We…met before."

I whipped my head to look at her and back to the road as quickly as I could without killing us. "What do you mean?"

"I went to La Vista high school."

La Vista sounded familiar. I'd been to so many, they ran together. "It's in Collier," she explained.

"Oh, yeah. You did?" I was beyond shocked. Not only did I not remember her at all, but that was junior year. The year I learned that being a jerk kept me safe from any girls that would care and put me in the arms of all the ones that didn't. I got nervous. Crap, if she was there, then there was no telling what she saw.

"I can't believe you haven't told me until now," I deflected.

"Don't get all fidgety," she said, but she didn't laugh. "I know you were a different person then. I know who you are now. I…recognized you at the party that night, but you were same…jerk you'd been before, except this time, you were actually interested in *me*."

Ah, hell…she *had* seen something awful.

"What did I do?" I whispered.

I faced forward. I couldn't look at her as she fished in my past, reminding me of things I did that I was sure I was going to regret even more now.

"You misunderstood me." She smiled sadly, I could hear it. "You were…entertaining…some girls in front of my locker. I came up to you, in all my freshman glory, and tried to ask you to move, but-"

The scene played out in front of my eyes and I remembered. And I could see it now. It was her and I'd been such an ass, assuming that she was hitting on me…when she'd just been trying to get into her locker. I remember her gorgeous face and the destroyed look I'd put on it.

She was still talking, telling me it was OK.

I looked over my right shoulder, seeing no one, and cut across all four lanes of traffic to slam to a stop in a back parking spot at the rest stop. My breaths heaved. I still hadn't looked at her. I didn't know if I could. I remembered her face, her look of just utter hurt at what I'd said to her-not just said it, but did it in front of other people. Those girls, those stupid bullies who thought they were better than everybody. Then I just left a few weeks later, leaving Marley to that school and that life. The college wasn't very far from that school. Over the years, I'd made my way back.

She'd been right there, my salvation, and I'd practically spit in her face.

I felt her hand on my jaw, forcing me to look at her. I didn't want to, but I obeyed. She looked at me with sympathy, not disgust. "What the hell did I do to deserve that look?"

"You changed."

"Marley…" I choked. Holy…I was about to lose it.

She crawled into my lap, fitting snugly between my hips and the steering wheel. She took my face in her hands and kissed my lips once. "I didn't tell you that so you'd get upset, I just wanted to tell you. I don't like secrets and this felt like one. It's why I was so angry with you in the beginning. I thought…you would always be that guy and when you didn't remember me…" she scoffed, "that made the sting even worse."

"Marley," I tried again. "I'm so, so sorry. I was so messed up back then with anger. It was the hardest time in my life because I wasn't a cute kid anymore so people stopped helping me so easily. I had to start working and trying to save money on my own and… Girls were always asking me to ask them out and…even though it was what I wanted at the time, using people and being used made me an angry, bitter person. It's not an excuse."

"It's not," she agreed. "I understand. You looked at me like every other girl in that place that tried to use you."

"But you weren't trying to use me." I gulped. "You just wanted your freaking books. And I...humiliated you."

"A little." She smiled. "But I got over it. And soon enough, I moved and was on to another foster home. I really just wanted to tell you this so you'd see how our paths have crossed. More than once. For whatever reason..." She lifted her hands to suggest the sky, "Whatever this is. We were meant to find each other, to find the men responsible for our mothers and get them some justice."

I shook my head. "I was meant to find *you*."

She bit her lip. "I was meant to be found."

I pulled her mouth down to me and tried to tell her how sorry I was with these lips. God...to live a life so carelessly and think you're not hurting anyone but yourself...

I placed my hand on the small of her back and pressed her to me. Our hips lined up, igniting a growl from me. She gasped into my mouth and wrapped her arms around my head to bring us closer. My hands wanted some new territory for this occasion and started to go south, but I remembered her past and didn't want to scare her with that yet.

Before I could think, she reached back and placed them right on her behind. I huffed a laugh into our kiss and used my newfound backside real estate to grip, tug, and pull at her.

She leaned my head back and kissed the spot under my ear, making good on her promise. My mouth fell open in silent groan and my grip tightened on her. My breathing was so ragged that the windows were fogged. When she kissed my earlobe, I was done letting her have control and pulled her back to me.

She made the most amazing noises against my lips and by the time I was done with her, her lips were swollen and there was probably another hickie around there somewhere.

I locked the door, content to stay in that truck with her all night. She didn't even ask, she just laid her head down in the crook of my neck and let me lull her to sleep.

While I stayed up that night facing my demons, I felt another ray of sunshine blow through my soul as the girl on my lap murmured my name in her sleep.

It didn't matter how much time had passed, I was in love with this girl and I knew it because she was breaking me. Like a block of ice chipped away with an ice pick, she wielded that blade with precision. I was at her mercy and she wasn't letting the blows slow. And the strangest, most amazing part about it?

I didn't want to run. Not at all.

I smiled a full on genuine smile and finally went to sleep.

The next day, I drove straight through again and we finally reached New Mexico late that night. We decided not to sleep in the truck and found a single-level motel to stay in.

I brought all the papers in and combed them once more to try to find something important we may have missed while Marley took a hot bath. I tried to think of the best course of action for the next day. Should I wait until nighttime before trying to get in? Should I just go and ask to speak to someone about it? I didn't think that would work since they had people chasing us.

I finally gave up and realized the Chinese food guy had delivered over twenty minutes ago and she was still in the tub.

I knocked and heard her soft, "Come in."

I peeked to see her buried under a sea of bubbles. I smiled. "Are you pruny yet? Food's here."

"Yes," she sighed, "but I kinda have a headache. I need to wash my hair though."

I looked around and grabbed the shampoo off the counter. But I didn't give it to her. I leaned down and touched her forehead while her eyes were closed. "You all right?"

"Yeah, it's just a headache."

I stood and rolled up my pant legs. "Sit up," I told her.

"Why?" she whispered as if speaking hurt, but saw me climb in behind her, my legs in the water, and me sitting on the tub deck. She just watched me.

I poured shampoo in my hand and waited for her to turn back around. She did with a little smile, wrapping her arm around my leg. I washed and massaged her head and scalp for so long my own hands were pruny.

"Better?" I asked, moving and rubbing down to her shoulders.

"Yes. Thank you," she groaned. She moved her hand down to my ankle. "You have sexy feet."

I snickered. "Uh...OK."

"I'm serious. You don't believe me?" She smiled, turning a little. "Don't ever wear flip-flops. You'll cause a riot."

I laughed and got out, drying off. "Sure. Girls don't think feet are sexy. Guys do, but not girls."

I looked down at her, my girl all covered in suds.

My girl…

"I am a girl and I say your feet are sexy," she argued as she looked at them over the tub side.

I squirmed and laughed. "Cut it out."

She pulled the shower curtain to and stood. "OK. I'm done. Hand me the towel?"

Before I could hand it to her, the bathroom door opened, revealing our neighbor from before. My friendly helper guy who was actually working with Biloxi. My fists tightened and I got ready for a fight. He held his hands up like he was surrendering, but I didn't buy it.

"What the hell are you doing here?"

I heard Marley peek out and gasp, jerking the curtain closed again to hide herself.

"I know what it looks like," he began.

"We know all about BioGene."

His eyes bulged on cue. I handed Marley the towel over the top. "How do you know-"

"You don't worry about that. I don't know what you want with us-"

"I'm not here to hurt you."

"You're just following us for…what?"

He sighed. "I'm one of you."

"One of us?" Marley asked. She opened the curtain a little with the towel wrapped around her. I growled and stood in front of her. Was she crazy?

"Yes, one of you. If you know about BioGene, I imagine you know that we were…experiments."

"For what?"

"All kinds of stuff. But that's not important. I know you've been running for a long time, but you don't have to. We don't want to hurt you, we want to help you."

"Help us what? We were fine until you started following us and trying to run us down in cars."

He shook his head. "If you remember right, I didn't hurt you. In fact, I helped her get you to the hospital."

So he did.

"So now what?"

"We want to bring you in for your own safety."

"From who?"

"There are a few of us that don't agree with the way some things were done."

"What happened to your mother?" I asked, changing the subject and seeing what he was made of. He didn't blink.

"She died during my birth. I was raised by nurses in the facility."

I paused. "Facility?"

"Yes. Where your mothers lived for almost a year."

What? I looked back at Marley and she looked as confused as I felt. I gripped her hand and she squeezed.

"OK, first things first," I told him. "Get out so she can get dressed. Then we'll talk."

He nodded with chagrin and backed out, going to stand in front of the window. I grabbed some clothes for her and placed them on the counter. I turned to face the bathroom door, not leaving her alone, and she dressed quickly. She asked me a hundred hushed questions. Did I believe him. Did I want to run. Did I understand what he was telling us.

I calmed her, rubbing my hands down her arms. "Don't worry. We'll figure everything out."

She was gripping my shirt front, letting me comfort her, when the room behind me exploded in gunshots. I peeked out the sliver to see him being gunned down.

Biloxi.

But…how? He worked for them. Why would they kill him? I urged a silent Marley to the window over the toilet. She was shaking so badly, I wasn't sure she'd make it.

It was scarily like the day my mom and I escaped through the bathroom window. "I'll go first to catch you," I insisted. I climbed onto the toilet seat and out the window easily, landing on my feet. It was a bit of a drop, but manageable. I coaxed her down. "Come on, baby. Hurry. I've got you."

When she climbed down, her behind rubbed against my neck and down my entire body. I gripped her sides to ease her down and didn't even get a chance to enjoy any of it because she was shaking so badly and I was so scared that someone was about to hurt her like they hurt my mom.

But I didn't plan to allow that to happen this time.

No longer a boy who lost it all, I was a man that realized how much I had to lose.

I took her hand and we took off running. I stuck my head around the building, but our truck was surrounded by men. I cursed and looked around. Downtown was only about half a mile. We could make it on foot and...I didn't know. I'd decide that later.

I took her hand and pulled her with me. We ran to the fence and I linked my fingers together to hoist her over. She climbed down the other side and I scaled it quickly. We were both barefoot, but it could be worse.

"Jude, what are we doing?" she hissed and lifted one foot. "There's stuff in the grass."

"Get on," I ordered, bending down for her to climb on my back.

"What about your feet?"

"Get on, sweetheart," I said quickly. "I'm fine."

She climbed on and I gripped her legs under her knees, walking swiftly. We were silent and Marley was still shaking slightly. We made it to the first gas station and I put her down as we walked in the door. I bought us each a pair of cheap flip-flops that had the picture of the state of New Mexico on the sole and a keychain-sized pepper spray for Marley.

She gripped it tightly and gave me a look. "Hopefully, you won't need it, sweetheart, but just in case."

"I love it when you call me that," she whispered as she looked out into the dark road. "We're going to find the facility or whatever now, aren't we?"

"Yes. I'm going to buy you a bus ticket and then I'll come when I get everything all-"

"Oh, my gosh. Are you out of your mind!" she screeched.

"Hey!" we heard from behind us. I looked at the gas station attendant. "Take it outside. No fighting in the store."

She took off in a huff and I followed her. Down the side highway, she walked angrily with me beside her. "I can't believe you're dumping me after all."

THIRTEEN

"I'm not dumping you," I promised. "Do you realize I'm going to have to break in? I just don't want you to get hurt."

"I'm not some little woman that needs to be taken care of. I've done just fine without you for my whole life, Jude! I'm not fragile."

"Yes, you are!" She stopped on the sidewalk and looked at me. I tried to tone it down. "You are fragile and you are a woman who needs to be taken care of." She started to protest, but I moved and took her face in my hands. "You *deserve* to be taken care of. You've done a great done job so far, but, sweetheart, there's nothing wrong with letting somebody take over for a while. Let me take care of you. Let me protect you. I know you've never had someone to look after you before, but now you do."

"Jude," she swallowed, "I'm coming with you." I gritted my teeth. "You can't do this by yourself. I need to see this for myself as much as you do."

"I want you safe."

"They ruined my life, too."

Dang…she had to throw that last jab. "Fine."

"Fine," she rebutted and we walked in silence.

I had to pat myself on the back for staying calm because right then, I was about five miles south of *fine*. I didn't want her anywhere near that place, but what was I going to do, tie her to a park bench?

I growled at the thought of them finding her.

"What are you growling about?" she spouted.

"I think you probably know." We made it to the highway and I looked for a taxi. I flagged one down, but he kept going.

"I don't know," she rebutted. I tried to flag another one down and she threw her arms up in exasperation. "Jude, this isn't New York. Taxis don't just pull over to pick people up in New Mexico."

I turned, growling at how badly this whole thing was going down, but stopped. A dark SUV pulled into the gas station we had just left and the man who got out was Biloxi. Three other men got out, too, and went inside. They left the car on. I could still hear the engine.

I didn't think. I grabbed Marley's hand and we ran to it, jumping in. I looked in the backseat, a quick glance, before locking the doors and slamming it into reverse. They saw their car leaving, but I was sure they couldn't see us in the dark car. I sped from the lot, looking back to see Biloxi punching and kicking one of the men. Probably the one driving.

Marley said my name in a quiver, "Jude." I looked over to see a gun in her hand. A silver handgun. "It was under the seat. Take it," she insisted. I did, seeing how many bullets were left, and checked to make sure the safety was on before sticking it in the back of my pants.

"The chamber's full."

"You got your gun after all. So...we're doing this."

I peeked at her as we sped down the interstate. "This ends tonight." I took her hand and held it tight as I said the next words. Wow, I was becoming a chick. "I understand why you needed to come." She looked at me with no anger. "I do. I just hate the idea that I'm bringing you to the danger instead of waiting for it to find us. But I'll protect you. No matter what."

"I'm not worried. Everything seems to be pulling us there. Even this car." She pointed to the NAV and went to saved searches. The address of the facility was in there and she pressed for it to take us there. "See."

"All right. We're doing this. Stay low, stay behind me, and if we come across somebody, just act like you're supposed to be there."

"Like we're the cleaning people or something?"

I smiled. "That works for me."

"We're wearing flip-flops, Jude. I don't think there are any positions that would let us wear flip-flops."

I laughed, but it was laced with all sorts of feelings. This was it. I was finally going to figure out what happened to my mom, why she was always running with me, and why they were after us.

I glanced over at Marley and could see her wheels turning, too. I squeezed her hand and she looked at me with a sad smile. "Either way, we'll know," she said and wiped one tear from her eye.

I nodded. "Either way, sweetheart. This is it."

It took us about two and a half hours to get there. It was late and the compound was dark, all except one wing. There was a gate around the entire building and parking lot, but it was open. We went in and I stiffened when a guard who was sitting by the front door stood. He looked closely at the car and then waved us on from afar, content to go back to his seat.

Well, that was easy.

I pulled around back and we parked for a minute to look things over. The place was kind of small and disappointing. This was headquarters and I figured it would have been bigger or more…bigger.

"Should we ring the bell?" Marley spouted.

I smiled. "Hold your horses. We need to figure out how to get in. The fence may have been open, but I seriously doubt the door will be.

A car pulled in behind us and a scraggly man got out quickly, juggling his coffee and folders while he sprinted to the door. I watched his hand for the code.

He went in and I looked around before I got out. She followed suit and we walked to the door. I punched in what I thought was the code, but it didn't work. It beeped to let us know that we got it wrong. "Oh, thanks, door, for stating the obvious."

She giggled and sighed. She punched in a code, only one number different from mine and the door clicked. I yanked it open and looked at her like she stole my thunder. "Men," she scoffed. "You need to get glasses, by the way. You're welcome!" she sang in a whisper.

I clicked the door shut and we stared at a long, white corridor with multiple doors. "What is this, the freaking Matrix?" she asked.

I looked at her, slack-jawed. Now she was a Matrix movie buff?

God had sent this girl to me.

She started to inch down the hall. I took her hand and moved her behind me, giving her a look that said what my mouth didn't dare. Her look said, *Fine, whatever*. I started to go, but stopped. I turned and with my hand on her jaw, brought her to me. One kiss to take with me to whatever fate waited for us down this hall.

She licked her lips and blinked a few rapid times. I nodded to tell her it was go time.

We inched down the hall to find room after room of glass-walled, empty offices. They had desks in them and chairs, but looked to be empty. Looked like no one had ever even used them. We searched the entire place and found not one piece of paper, not one soul. I was so confused.

We had just seen that guy come in. There had to be something we were missing.

So we started backtracking and I almost missed it for a second time. The stairwell door was white as well as the walls. I told her to be quiet as I eased the door open. There was no squeak and we went in. The door shut and then we heard it bolt into place. Marley tried to open it, but it wasn't budging. They were obviously trying to keep anyone without a code from getting inside. I imagined my mom in a place like this, locked in…

I went first down the stairs and came to the bottom. It was just one level. I eased it open and peeked into the hall to see another long hallway with doors. We went and searched for anything that would help. This was it. We were there.

Marley's breathing was getting ragged behind me and I gripped her fingers tighter. I knew she was scared, but she was also tough as hell.

I pulled us to a stop in front of a room labeled **Observation Room.** I felt my skin crawl at the sound of that, but we inched inside. I gasped at what I saw.

The room was big and shaped like a horseshoe, but the part that made my heart stop was what was below us. There, in small walk-in closet-sized spaces, were a bed and a dresser. And room after room was a child.

Marley gasped and pressed her hand to the glass above one boy's room. He couldn't have been more than five years old, but even when she knocked on the glass, he didn't look up. "It's one-way glass," I told her.

"Jude," she whimpered and looked back at me, helplessly. "What are we gonna do?"

I looked at them all, nothing the same or different about them. There was no rhyme or reason, no pattern or gender to explain it. There were nine in all, four boys and five girls.

I searched the room for anything. There was only one computer in the corner and it was blinking a picture of a globe with a DNA strand around it like a planet ring. I touched the mouse and the brightly lit home screen popped up. There were so many files on the desktop, so I just double clicked one. There were a lot of links inside that only had dates to differentiate. It was a video, a woman. A date flashed above her head the entire time along with the letter C. She was explaining how her pregnancy was going, how she wasn't sick, that she felt great and energized, her feet hadn't swollen any, and she had no reason to know she was pregnant at all except for the bulging belly. She laughed at that.

I knew something bad was coming.

I clicked further down to a later date and she was still chipper and telling them her details as a deep voice asked her specifics off camera. But at the end of the video, she asked about seeing her father again. She said, "I don't understand why it's so hard. Why can't I just call him?"

"You'll disrupt the experiment. No electronics of any kind are to be within ten feet of you and the baby."

"So put him on speaker phone. I just want to talk to him. He'll be worried if I don't call. It's been months."

"He knew you were going to a secret location to help your country with an experiment. He'll understand."

"I just don't see why-"

"Miss Core. That's enough for today."

"Can I please have something to do other than crossword puzzles?"

"No electronics," he repeated harder.

"It doesn't have to be." She sat on the bed, looking tired emotionally, but physically, she looked pretty amazing. "Just something else."

"I'll see what I can do."

Even I knew that was a crock.

The camera stopped and I clicked a later date. I sat in the chair there and pulled a quiet Marley into my lap. We needed to see, but I knew it was going to hit too close to home. Our mothers probably had a video just like this somewhere.

I clicked the very last date in the file and Marley gasped, covering her mouth. I wrapped my arms around her and stared at the shell of a woman on the screen. She was weeping, banging her fists on the glass like she'd been doing it for hours, days even, with no results. She was mumbling something I couldn't understand. I slowly turned the volume up until we could make out the pleas of the mother before us.

"Give me back my baby."

FOURTEEN

Marley turned, shaking and whimpering into my shoulder. She didn't want nor need to look anymore, but *I* had to. She didn't know what her mother looked like and to her, that could have been her mother. But I knew mine, and I needed to see. But first…

"That wasn't her, baby," I assured into her hair. "That wasn't her."

"It could've been, Jude." She sniffed, trying to keep it together. "We'll never know which one was her."

The woman on the video had been dark olive skinned and my girl was pale and blond like a porcelain doll. There was no way that woman was her mother, but the not knowing was torturing her.

I wish to all that was holy that she had let me save her from this by getting on that bus.

I stood, scooting her up so I could pass, and went to find the kid. I just knew since the dates weren't as far back that he or she was there. I looked and it didn't take long to match the dark hair and skin to a little Mediterranean beauty below us.

She was wearing a plain white smock or hospital gown with no socks or shoes and couldn't have been more than eight. There was no TV or radio or anything in the room. She sat on the bed and sang some song that I couldn't hear. I beckoned Marley to me and she rushed to the window. It was obvious this girl was her daughter and not Marley because of the dates I saw, but Marley was on a mission that was a little different from mine.

She wanted to know what happened to her mom to make her throw Marley away.

I went back and pressed lots of those folders and links to see if I could find my mom, but couldn't. There was just too many of them and we needed to get to the room with all the information. Files, records, whatever. We got that there was some shady experiments going on, but we needed to know why.

The last link I clicked was an older date, a couple years before I was born, and I went to one of the last links in the folder. She was talking to the wall for all I knew. No one appeared to be there, but she was confessing everything. I realized who she was confessing to when she gripped her huge belly and cried as she spoke.

"Oh, God…I didn't know. They said they'd help me. They said if I helped them with their experiment, it would all be paid for and I'd be helping people, too. But it's not that at all. I'm so sorry. I've killed you by bringing you here. I've killed myself. They won't let us stay together. You'll be all alone. I'm so sorry, baby."

I turned off her mumbling and took a deep breath. That was it, wasn't it? Mom had gotten pregnant, the douche probably ran like cowards do, and she was all alone. She would never tell me about my dad. They came, told her they'd help her if she helped them. I'm sure they made it sound like a Godsend in her time of need. When she found out what was going on, she ran somehow, got away, and we never stopped running.

I took another breath. God…my chest hurt thinking about her doing all that for me. Just so I'd never know what it was like to grow up in a room all by myself like those kids down there.

We heard a door and looked up to see a man in a doctor's coat enter one of the children's rooms. We couldn't hear them. I searched, knowing there had to be a way for us to hear them in an observation room, and found a button that turned on the speakers.

He told the boy, "…and the test will begin just as they always do. We'll poke your finger, put the blood on a piece of glass, and then we'll take a hair sample and a swab from the inside of your cheek. And then if that works, then…tomorrow they'll come and take a little marrow."

"No!" he yelled and backed away from him. "Please don't do that. It hurts."

"I know it hurts," the man placated, "but don't you want to help people? Don't you want to save people's lives?"

"Yes, but why do I have to be awake when you hurt me?"

The man cleared his throat. "That's the only way it can be done." The boy wiped his eyes, clearly not happy. "And they won't do any more tests on you for a week. How's that?"

The boy didn't answer and I imagined myself in the room below, waiting to be harvested for bodily fluids. I felt my eyes sting with angry tears.

Then the man left and went a couple doors down to another boy's room. He went through the same spiel as he had with the other boy except he looked at his chart and instead of taking bone marrow, they were taking his spleen.

His freaking spleen.

Marley was keeping her soft cries to herself as she covered her mouth.

I turned away. I couldn't watch anymore. I searched the room and the computer for anything new that might help us, and when I found nothing, I towed Marley into the hall.

She was quiet, as was I. I didn't want to think about those kids being down there for another second, but first, we had to get our evidence. The hall twisted and turned and I tried to remember which way we'd gone so we didn't get lost. We never saw a soul. I started opening doors and looking in them to see what was what.

We found more rooms with beds, but they were empty, a lab with humming machines and hospital beds, a small nursery...

Finally, we came upon a room full of computers, file shelves, and desks. It wasn't labeled, but we assumed it was the records room.

I sat at one of the computers while Marley got to work going through files. "These are patient charts, Jude."

"Oh, good," I said. "That will probably be great for-"

"No," she said, panicked. "Jude...these are patient charts." Her voice shook and I followed her eyes, gulping. The wall was lined, floor to ceiling, at least ten feet long with files for patients. So many people... How did no one know about this? How did they justify all those missing people?

I cursed and closed my eyes. This was bigger than some company with a couple offices in the city. This was…an operation.

She started tearing through them, looking for anything. But again, we didn't even know exactly what we were looking for. "These were all pregnant, Jude," she muttered softly.

I started going through files on the computer, financial records, contributions, donations, some people had even donated their body to the organization for scientific purposes. I'd never heard of this company, but in the scientific and medical circles, it was obviously a big deal.

Then, under the financials was a payroll listing. I found a USB stick already in the computer and started to put the most important things on it, that being one of them. If we made it out, the cops would have a list of all the people who worked there, all the people that they needed to arrest for murder. There was no way someone worked there and didn't know what was going on.

The job titles were all these medical professions that I couldn't even pronounce. Then I started putting the list of *Test Subjects* on the drive, too. I was sure there were plenty of missing persons cases this could help solve.

Then there were some company files, mission statements, meeting dictations, all sorts of things that I didn't have time to weed through. I didn't put those on the drive for fear of me finding something else more important that needed to fit on it.

I went back to the *Test Subjects* file. Then I gritted my teeth at what I found. A subfolder titled *Terminated*. Inside, the list was long and next to each name was a letter—a room letter I assumed— and then it said either *Deceased* or *Terminated*. I knew what the difference meant. I searched for my mom's name. It said *Terminated* by it. I clicked on the JPEG beside it and there she was. All vibrant and alive in a way that I never really knew her. And I felt like that little boy again, watching her die in front of my eyes.

Then I let my eyes search for Marley's mom's name, I prayed it said deceased. But it didn't. They had killed hers like they killed mine. The date for her death was when Marley would have been three years old. I looked at her and she knew.

"You found something about her, didn't you?"

"How old were you when she...gave you up."

"Three years, two months, and nine days. But who's counting?" She smiled sadly. "Just tell me."

I waited. I clicked on the picture of her and an older version of my Marley popped up. Her hair was longer, her skin somehow paler, and she was giving this little, shy smile. I closed my eyes and hated this. "Come here, sweetheart."

She came slowly and when she saw her mom's face for the very first time, I watched as her world shattered. I was sure it was nothing like she pictured her. She covered her face, everything but her eyes, and stared at the woman who gave her up to save her.

As she sobbed and realized her mom had loved her so much that she died for her, I held her tightly. She wrapped her arms roughly around my neck and held on. I soothed her the only way I was learning how to, by being there. I let my hands say what my lips didn't know how to and pressed her to me, rubbing her skin in circles under her shirt.

I wasn't sure how long we stood like that, but we needed to get moving. I hated to interrupt her when she needed this time to grieve, but I had to. I lifted her face, smoothed her cheeks of tears, and hoped to hell that she was going to be all right. I knew what guilt looked like—I'd had years to deal with mine—but hers was just now hitting her full-force. "I'm so sorry, baby."

She nodded. "Me, too."

"We've got to go."

She nodded again. "I know."

I turned back to the computer and printed the picture of her mom off for her. I took it from the printer on the back desk, folded it, and stuck it in her back pocket for her. I kissed her once.

"Thank you for finding her," she whispered.

I didn't feel like I deserved any thanks. On our way out, she stopped me and said that we should take our mothers' files with us. We looked, but couldn't find them. They were in order of date, so we looked for our birthdays, but that didn't match up. Then I realized it wasn't their birthdays or ours, it was by their *Terminated* date. Sure enough, we found both folders that way.

Marley stuffed them both into the back of her pants and let her shirt cover them. That was a good thing because as soon as I opened the door, we came face-to-face with a man that didn't look happy to see us there.

"How did you get in here?" he asked, truly perplexed.

I reached for my gun slowly and told him, "You were the guy in there with that little boy."

His eyes widened and he huffed. "How long have you been here? How did you get in?" He reached for something in his pocket, but I was faster on the draw.

"Nuhuh, big boy. Hands up."

"Are you a terrorist?" he asked, glancing down the hall nervously. "Our anthrax isn't the kind you can weaponize, you know."'

"I'm not here to steal your anthrax." I pushed him to the wall, the gun under his chin. I saw a ring on his finger. "Married? Got kids?"

"Yes," he stuttered and seemed to get an idea. "Yes, I have three beautiful, talented little girls who would miss their daddy very much. Please, let me go."

I scoffed. "So because your kids are *talented* you're worth more than other daddies? Is that what you're saying?"

Marley stuck behind me, her fingers gripping my shirt. "No...yes, maybe. I don't know!" he roared. "You've got a gun in my face!"

"So you would never want anything to happen to them, would you? Like being put in a room for the rest of their lives and harvested for organs! Or plasma and blood." My lividness reached maximum capacity. "You sick bastard!"

I reared back and punched him with the fist not holding the gun. It was my left for crying out loud, but he went down like a sack of onions and cried like he'd been chopping some, too. I jerked him up by his collar. "Get up. We're going for a walk and you're going to tell us everything."

"Everything about what?"

He tripped and I made him stand. "About our mothers and what you were doing with them."

"Your mothers?" He tried to look back confused, but I made him walk. "I don't know your mothers. I would know their room number and last name. That's all. We don't make things personal around here. Just professional."

I scoffed louder. "Why? To keep your conscience clean?"

He didn't answer, lucky for him. I shoved him back into the observation room and pushed him into the chair. I put the gun back into my pants because I could see this guy was a pansy and would cause no trouble. I told Marley to let him see the picture of her mom. She did, her fist closed tight. The man shook his head. "I don't know her. I wasn't working here then, but if you were the children of women in this facility, then that means…"

He was interrupted by the door opening behind us. It revealed a rather large man and three other men carrying rifles. They were in uniforms like security guards, but he was in a black suit. The security guards looked pretty pissed. I smirked. "You got chewed out, huh?" I tacked on a wink for good measure.

One of them stepped forward like he was going to bust my teeth, but the man barked for him to stand down. He smiled at us. "Look, I'm sure there's some logical explanation for all of this. Let's just sit down and we'll work it all out, yeah?"

He told the lab coat to get lost, then ticked his head out the door. One of them grabbed my arm to drag me down the hall. But that meant... I looked back to see the shortest one snatch Marley in front of him. When I heard her gasp, I saw red. I slammed my elbow into my guy's nose, actually smiling when I heard it crunch, and went for Marley's. He didn't stand a chance as my fists connected with his chin. He went down and I pulled Marley to me. The other two jumped on me quick and one rifle butt went into my gut and the other the back of my head.

I hit the floor, hearing Marley's scream. I shook my head and blinked as I rolled over. One of them had his arm around Marley's neck as she looked down at me. I made myself get up for another go-round.

The suit took one of their rifles and shot it into the ceiling once, halting us all. "Hey, hey, hey!" he yelled. "All right, let's all just calm down."

"Get your hands off her right now or you'll be eating that arm," I threatened the man with Marley. The suit could shoot me, but I wasn't going to watch as she was hurt anymore by these people.

The suit told the guy to let her go. He glared at him, but did so. She bolted to me and wrapped one arm around my middle, while the other inspected the back of my head, turning my face. "Oh, my gosh," she whispered.

She turned to them. "He's hurt. He's bleeding because of you."

"He's bleeding because he broke into my building," the suit countered.

I squeezed Marley, hoping she understood not to say anything. I was thinking it was a better idea for this guy to make his own assumptions about why we were there. If he found out we were returnees, he might decide playtime in the operating room wasn't over for us. Who knew what the hell these people would do.

"Come into my office. That's not a request," he said, pointing at me with his gaze. "You broke in, I didn't bring you here. I don't know what you're after, but I'm sure we can keep the police out of it if we just calm down."

I shook my head. Of course he wanted to keep the police out of it. They were murdering people and who knew what else. But he thought we were common thieves. So we followed him, arms around each other. I tried to let her know it was all going to be OK, but we just stared at each other. They held the door for us and pushed us to sit down on a small couch in the corner of the room.

"Now," he asked, leaning on the edge of his desk, "what is it that you were after, how did you get in here, and how did you know we had what you wanted to begin with?"

I looked at the door, but shorty was guarding it. So, I told the truth, mostly. I told them we figured they were a medical facility and would have anything we wanted and we waited, watching the guy put the code in. Then we just walked in because there was no one around.

"Yes," he drawled and gave the men a look, "apparently football was more important than intruders." He smiled at me. "The Patriots beat the pants off the Jets, by the way."

"Ah, come on, man!" I complained.

He laughed. "It was ruined for me. It was only fair to ruin the game for someone else." He watched us. "Now, what to do with you?"

Marley shook in my arms. I rubbed her arm to soothe her, but it was pointless. I had let her down.

"Are you hungry? Thirsty?" he asked and I told him a firm no. I didn't want any poison they had to offer. "All right, well as I said, we'll leave the police out of this. Nothing was stolen yet, so no harm, no foul."

I didn't smile. I didn't trust this guy as far as I could toss him. He looked between us several times before standing. "All right, well we're gonna go chat for a sec. Sit tight." He winked and grinned as he left. He wasn't letting us go. He knew it and I knew it.

I sighed. I couldn't look at Marley as I spoke. I was strangely calm for someone who was probably about to no longer walk this earth. I was just...spent.

"I'm so sorry, Marley." I played with her fingers on my knee just to keep touching her, to remember exactly what it felt like. "I don't know what to do to fix this."

She smiled sadly and reached up, touching my lips with her thumb. "It's not your fault."

"No, it is my fault that I couldn't protect you."

She took a shaky breath. "I'm not your responsibility, Jude. I'm just a girl who got dumped on you." She looked down at her lap.

"A girl that I adore," I corrected.

"A girl you adore that you're stuck with because you're a gentleman and you...you won't..."

I shook my head, my brow low. "Marley." I moved until I was right up against her, or she was right up against me. I bent a little while pulling her chin up, making her look me right in the eye. "Don't you know?"

"Know what?" Her enraptured voice made me swell with happiness that she wanted me, too.

"That you're mine."

She blinked rapidly, the corners of her mouth lifting. Before she could say anything, the door swung open again…to reveal Biloxi.

I jumped up, shoving Marley behind me. He smiled at me. Or…at Marley. "Marley, you've finally made your way back to us."

I frowned at that. He continued. "Come on, honey. You've done your job. You got him here and that's all we wanted."

The blood rushed in my ears. What did he just say? Marley wasn't denying it. I turned slowly to find her open-mouthed and looking at me strangely. What the hell…

"Marley?" I questioned and finally, she opened her mouth.

"Jude, no, I'm not with him."

He laughed sadly. "Come on. The jig is up. You don't have to pretend anymore… Oh, no." He looked between us and sagged a little in defeat. "Good Lord, you fell for him, didn't you?"

"Yes," she whispered and looked at me, only me. "Yes, I

fell for him." She shook her head. "Jude, you can't believe him. After everything that happened, you believe him?"

I stared. I didn't believe him, not really. There had been too much that was real. Too much that was raw. I shook my head. She gripped my fingers in her hands, distracting me, when I felt the crack on my skull.

I went down, my head on the floor, and watched her adorable toes scramble away as my vision disappeared and sleep claimed me.

FIFTEEN

I woke, the smell of pepper choking me and burning my nose. I opened my eyes, only to be assaulted there, too. I looked around the room, sitting up and immediately regretting it, and saw Marley's pepper spray on the floor. The air was coated with it so she must have used it.

Which meant they'd taken her and she tried to get away.

Good girl.

"Mother…" I groaned as I stood and felt the back of my head. There was a lot of blood, but I had to find her. I felt the back of my pants and the gun was there. I left it there, keeping my hand on the handle, but finger off the trigger, and inched into the hallway.

I leaned on the hall wall and made my way down. My head pulsed and my vision went in and out in blurs. I made myself keep going faster. When I heard a door slam behind me, I slid quickly into an alcove. I heard someone yell, the echo carrying it down the hall. "He's not here!"

I squeezed my eyes shut. If only I had gotten further away before they found out. I heard one say he was going this way and for the other guy to go that way. I listened and when his running footsteps almost reached me, I threw half of my body out, slinging my arm straight and tightening it. His neck slammed into it, effectively close-lining him as I'd been trying to do. He went down hard, choking on my arm, and the thud as his head hit the tile didn't sound encouraging that he'd get up again. I took his gun, slinging the strap over my shoulder, and then picked up his radio. I tried every channel, but heard nothing.

I turned to the double doors in the alcove and pushed them open as I didn't have anywhere else to go. I pulled his body into the room so no one would see him.

I wanted to look for Marley, not get into a shootout. Not yet anyway. I blinked in the bright lights and looked around the empty room. It was a lab. Patient charts were lined up on a rack behind a bunch of medical stuff and supplies that I knew nothing about. I leaned on the table for support and pulled one down. No patient name, only the letter D and a date.

I shook my head. The bastards couldn't even call them by their names.

The chart was handwritten notes, pages of them.

...alert and vital signs good. Was asked to walk...

...blood drawn. Patient showed mild discomfort...

...platelets counted. Procedure discussed...

...child was shown pictures of the disease...

...told male child others would die if he didn't...

...bone marrow. Patient will be awake for...

...child wanted to save others, but not give blood...

...child kept asking for mother. Was told she left...

On and on it went, page after page, chart after chart. They were taking blood, marrow, and organs from those kids and then testing them, using the research to make drugs, vitamins, and medicine for sick people was what I could get from it. Kids seemed to be the ones they wanted to experiment on most... But they wouldn't...

I slammed the charts down, catching my breath as I held on. That would have been me. That would have been Marley.

I went through to the next lab with the connecting door. I was starting to feel a little dizzy. I poked my head back out into the hall and, finding no one, went back down the hallway, listening as I went for voices so I could find her.

Why did they take her? What did they want with her now? She was an adult. I went up and down the main hall twice and didn't hear anything. I prayed she was still there and they hadn't left the compound with her. I'd never get her back.

My walkie crackled to life. I turned it down and pressed it to my ear to hear him. *"Michaels give your ETA, over."*

I groaned. I put my mouth on the speaker, thought fast, and talked deeply, "Male target in my custody on the first floor. He found a way up the stairs. Over."

Silence proceeded. And then, *"Why didn't you radio your position?"*

"Son of a bastard was fighting me hard."

"On our way. Detain for debriefing and termination. They don't need him, they've got the girl."

My heart stopped beating for a whole five seconds. No…Marley. "My orders were to bring him to the girl," I tried.

"Negative. Orders are to debrief and terminate. The girl will be taken to the Los Angeles facility for testing and creation."

Creation? I tried to chuckle into the mic, but it hurt my freaking soul to do it. "Well, dang. Sure was a pretty one. Was hoping she would stay for a while."

He laughed. *"She'll be back soon enough, Michaels. You still going to want her with a big ol' belly? Huh?"*

I froze. My hand gripped the radio so tight, I thought it might shatter. They were going to inseminate her and force her to have another experiment baby for them. Hell no. "You're right. No point anyway since they're just going to toss her afterwards."

"I thought that was your favorite kind?" he joked. *"Almost to your location. Over and out."*

I didn't answer the bastard. There was no telling what they'd done to the women staying there. Speaking of…where were the women? From the way they talked, they always had women in and out, so where were they? At another facility probably and I hated to think that.

Then I remembered those kids. I couldn't leave them. I needed to find Marley, but those kids… I dove back into the observation room to find it empty, but one of the rooms had several people in it.

"No," I heard myself say and pressed my hand to the glass to keep myself up. Lab coat guy had her strapped to the bed. She was being prepped for something and I remembered the button so I could hear them. I pressed it, coming back to the glass to see my handprint of blood from my head. I pushed all thoughts of that away—it didn't matter right then—and listened to him.

"...you see, the government wouldn't give us grants for what we needed because they said it was inhumane. My team of researchers wanted to be known for saving the world though! Use stem cells, they told us. But no, we needed live hosts, live cells, live bodies to test on."

The suit interrupted. "You thought we were looking for you to harm you. We just wanted to make sure you were safe. Your blood is dangerous," he hissed overdramatically. "My associate, Vincent, went too far in his antics to bring you both back, and but you see, you're the last two. None of the others who have ever escaped survived and we had to bring you back for you own safety and ours. We've steadily upped security measures, and we thought sending Tatum and him telling you that he was one of you would help coax you in, but...you're content to do things the hard way."

He patted her head, causing her to jerk as far from him as she could get. He left. The doctor bent down to her level. "See? You just don't know the things we're doing here to save lives, and you're a part of that!" he said excitedly.

"But you're killing people," she said, defeated. "How can you kill people to save others? How is that fair?"

"In the course of the program, the terminated only reach the thousands. About seventeen thousand to be exact from the very beginning. How are seventeen thousand people worth more than the billions we'll save with our new line of drugs?"

"You haven't cured anything!" she yelled at him. "Have you? Have you cured cancer? Have you cured Leukemia? Tell me what disease you've cured. Name it." He stared, twisting his lips. She shook her head and slammed it back to the mattress. "It's all trial and error and you're murdering people, no matter what you tell yourself."

"But it's not. We've helped pregnancies with our vitamins and have lots of promise with our anti-body boosting drugs. When you were a baby, you were full of the special vitamins given to you by your mother in the womb from the medicine she shook from us. Your blood could save lives if you just let us test on you. You just can't see it because you're strapped to the bed instead. You're thinking like a victim instead of a miracle that can save-"

"What if I was one of your daughters? Would you sacrifice her for the greater good?" She stared him down and I was so daggum proud of her.

He placed a chart on the table and left, just like that. Biloxi stood from the corner chair. I hadn't seen him there. When he turned where I could see his face, his eyes and cheeks were red and splotchy. He kept blinking and grimacing. I smiled. I couldn't help myself. My girl got Biloxi with her pepper spray.

When he rolled his sleeves up and pulled a tray out from under the table with tubes and needles, I knew his crazy side was coming out to play.

I backed away and darted out the door. I wasn't giving him the opportunity to hurt a hair on her. I wasn't going to let her down again. I ran, though I was dizzy, I ran. I pulled the gun from the back of my pants and pushed open the first door that was open. Empty. The next was locked. I didn't wait—I just shot the doorknob and took it hard with my shoulder.

As soon as I saw Biloxi's face, I stood straighter to get my aim right and fired two shots right into his chest. No begging, no pleading, no thinking. His eyes were so swollen from the pepper spray, he hadn't even seen me coming.

But I didn't feel a lick of guilt. The man had ruined my life, taken my mother from me, and was trying to take my girl. I couldn't even muster up a sigh for him.

I didn't know where the doctor was, but I was positive that he would coward away. I leaned down to unbuckle Marley's arms. I felt myself sway a little. She touched my cheek when she got one hand free. "I didn't think you were coming for me." I looked at her sharply, feeling as though she slapped me.

"You thought I'd just leave you?"

"I thought you believed him when he said I was... And then your head," she sobbed and touched my hair. "I thought you were..."

Her eyes were bloodshot, still wet from tears, and not from pepper spray. She really thought I wasn't coming back, for one reason or the more morbid one.

"Marley," I leaned my forehead to hers, "you belong to me. Remember?"

"Yes, I do," she countered with a sob.

I helped her off the table and knew first-things-first, we needed to find a phone and call the police. Then we needed to get those kids topside.

Before I could move, she pulled my face down to hers and kissed me so deeply. We both pulled and grabbed at each other like we never wanted to part again. I leaned back just barely, ran my thumb from her brow down to the tip of her nose and stopped at her lips, loving the way her eyes fluttered. "I'll always come to you."

She pressed her lips together and nodded. I took her hand, but before we left the room, I stared at Biloxi on the floor, his tray of needles and medicine bottles strewn around him. I never got to know why my mom or me for that matter was so important to him that he'd made it his life's work to kill us. It seemed like I'd never get the closure, never feel like it was finally over because I'd never know.

I kept Marley behind me as I took us back down the hall. If someone else decided to make an appearance, I wasn't sure I'd be able to fight them off. My vision was blurring and staying that way.

I heard her speaking, but couldn't focus on it. My ears were muffled or ringing. Then she touched my cheek, "Jude!" she hissed.

I focused on her face and it all stopped. "Huh?"

"I've been talking... Your pupils are dilated, Jude." She huffed an angry breath. "They..." She growled. "We've got to get you out of here."

"We can't leave those kids."

"We can't just walk them out of here either. We need to find a phone or..." she shrugged quickly, "I don't know. Something."

"I never saw any phones in the offices we were in. I bet we have to go topside for that. They wouldn't want them to have access to the outside."

She wrapped my arm around her shoulder. "Well, then let's go topside."

She started taking me the opposite way, past all the kid's rooms that I hadn't known were back there. "I saw a few of them go this way. We may run into some of them," she said and nodded to steel herself. "It'll be OK."

"Here," I told her. We stopped long enough for me to put the handgun in her hand and show her how to shoot the first round. "Just point and shoot."

"No cocking or loading or...swiveling something?"

I laughed, even in my state. "No, sweetheart. Not this one."

This must've been where the other wings were because we came upon another hallway of doors. I heard Marley's gasp as we passed the first room. They were doing a medical procedure on a small boy, maybe eight or nine. He was screaming, we could tell, but the soundproof glass kept the sound from us.

The awful image of his mouth in the shape of a painful, silent 'O' would be with me for the rest of my life.

The doctors were busy and hadn't heard or seen us, but the boy and Marley were staring at each other. Marley pressed her hands to the glass and failed at holding in a sob.

The doctor pulled a long needle from the boy's back and turned to see us. He looked at the other one and he ran for something. To press a security button, I was sure.

I raced him, opening the door and jamming my fist into his jaw and then his gut before he could make it to the red panic button by the door. The other one held his hands up, looking stricken, like we were the bad guys in this scenario. Marley helped the boy, putting the bandage they had laid out for him on, and helping him stand.

He didn't know Marley from Eve, but he clung to her and stared at the doctor, shivering so badly that his teeth were banging waiting for his next move. I couldn't help myself. I reared back and punched that doctor, too, but not enough to knock him out, just enough to piss him off and feel an ounce of what he'd done to that boy needlessly.

"We don't have money or drugs here, you stupid kids." He stood from where I'd knocked him and glared at me, holding his cheek. "We're not a hospital. We don't have pain meds here."

"Yeah," Marley spouted. "You torture your patients, so why would you need pain medicine?"

"Torture?" He shook his head. "No, little girl, you don't know what you're talking about. We are doing good work here."

"We know all about the mission statement," I spouted. "And that little boy just gave you his permission to poke and prod him?"

"His mother did-"

"For one," I cut in, "I highly doubt that, and two, you're an idiot if you believe that holding kids down and making them suffer is a respectable way to make a living."

"We are saving lives here, young man. We're gonna cure cancer someday."

"OK, so you *are* an idiot. What to do with you now?" I growled and lifted my gun a little. He gasped.

The doctor on the floor woke and yelled, "Stop! Don't! You can't hurt him! He's the best doctor we have and the only one who can perform the Mohs surgery to give the specialists the samples they need!"

I didn't know what Mohs surgery was, but if it gave the guy samples, I didn't think I wanted to know. But it did give me an idea.

I ticked my head toward the door, hoping I was hiding my pain well, and told the super special doctor to come with us. He glared at the doctor on the floor for the ammunition he'd given us. We thanked him by tying him to a steel table leg under the window line where no one would see him.

SIXTEEN

Marley held the boy's hand. He seemed embarrassed to be in a hospital gown and kept tugging at the back, but she assured him he was covered. As for the doc, well, he walked with my gun to his head. I told him we needed a phone and he said there was none.

I was barely holding on. He was so focused on the gun that he didn't realize I was about to keel over, but if he'd just get a real good look at me, he'd see. I blinked and opened my eyes wide to clear them. We passed a fire alarm on the wall as we exited the medical wing and into another hall. I told Marley to pull it. If it was hooked to the system like it should be, the fire department would come and so would the police.

The doctor showed the first signs of fighting back when he tried to stop her. I pressed the barrel to his cheek. "Wow, you really are an idiot, huh?"

"You don't realize what you're doing!" he roared just as she pulled it.

She had to beat the glass with the butt of the gun several times before it broke. She pulled it. The sirens went off in the form of red flashing lights on the ceiling and a whir so loud, my ears were ringing. The boy covered his ears, but Marley hugged him to her and looked around.

I dragged the doctor over with me to the rooms on that wing. We didn't know who were in those rooms, but we couldn't leave without checking. They were all locked and I was afraid to shoot at the door for fear of hitting them. Dang. We'd have to get topside and then get the police down there as soon as possible to let them out.

I started down the hall, leading the way, but Marley yelled my name. I stopped and she tried to yell over the siren, but I couldn't hear her. She pointed down the hall we'd just been from and I felt my heart lift at what we saw. The siren must have triggered a safety measure from the building's system. All the doors down the hall had unlocked and opened automatically and into the hall spilled several pregnant women along with more children and even some women that had babies in their arms.

I counted at least eleven. They all looked around curiously, and at seeing us, they understandably looked spooked. Marley raised her hands, pulling the boy who wouldn't let go with her, and tried to tell them something over the siren. I leaned my head back against the wall and closed my eyes.

I felt sick to my stomach. I needed to get out of here.

When I opened my eyes, Marley was coming back and looking at me worriedly. I shook my head at her. I didn't want the doc to know all he had to do was give me a good elbow and I'd be down for the count.

The women seemed on board so I led the way, opting to put the gun into his back instead so we could move faster. I yelled into his ear, "I will shoot you if you run. Don't think for a second that I won't."

Around the corner ran two minions and they skidded to a stop at seeing the doc with us. I put the gun into view at his head and they looked at each other before going back the way they came.

When we came to the kid's ward, I only hoped that pulling the alarm got the officials on the way. Things were underway now.

I wondered why they didn't just keep making the same women grow kids instead of getting new ones every time. It would seem, from a logical standpoint, that it would be easier to cover up less missing women.

As a huddle, with me leading the way, we trekked down the hall back to the stairs leading up topside. The last corner revealed the reason why I had started to think it was all too easy.

They were waiting for us.

He had somehow had the siren turned off and started talking, but my ears were ringing again and it took a few seconds to focus and catch up. The suit had a couple of his men with him, but the rest were leaving out the stairwell.

"So, you found our secret weapon." He seemed upset, but resolved. That scared me more than anything at that point. "You just had to come here, just had to know everything, didn't you?" He stepped forward three small steps and was so angry that he spit when he talked. "You just think you need to know everything. That it would ease you and tuck you in at night knowing that your mothers loved you. That by coming here and learning the truth that all the hurt would just flit away. You're fools. Vincent was justified to chase you so vigorously. He told me you'd be trouble. That by you being out there, you put our whole program in jeopardy. If anyone found out about what we do here, they would shut us down. They wouldn't understand the good things we're doing because they can't get past the gruesome parts that have to happen for cures to be found. You're not going to cure cancer by working on monkeys and mice. You want to cure human cancer, you need to study human subjects. We work very hard to keep everything under wraps. Your mothers escaping was a fluke, an accident, and we needed to correct it. Vincent was *the reason* your mother got away. It's why he chased her and now you so diligently." I felt my lips part at his statement. "She slipped right through his fingers, on his watch, but I won't be letting you. And then finding out that Marley, who we've also searched for all her life, was right there with you? It was as if we were destined to find you and bring you both here, back to where it all started. Fated to die so that others may live. I can't give you the chance to ruin all this. You two being alive is evidence against us." I was confused by that. "I won't allow it. I *can't* allow it."

I looked back at Marley. She was already looking at me. I turned back to the suit.

"Move. Let us through or your precious doctor paints the walls." I moved the gun to his temple. He whimpered.

"I'm sorry, Charles," he said. I realized he was talking to the doctor. "I can't risk the entire program for one man."

My arms spread with goosebumps at how calm his voice was.

"Paul," the doctored reasoned, "come now. Just let them go and all is fine."

"I can't let him go. Any of them. They all know too much."

Marley gasped, getting his meaning. The doctor pleaded, "You need me! You know you do."

"You're right. I do. And the program will suffer for a while until we find a replacement for you and all the test subjects, but…" He shrugged and stepped back. He pulled an old silver flip lighter from his pocket and lit it. The two guards with him pulled small, red cans from the side and began to pour. Gasoline… "It's what we have to do to keep things going. For the greater good."

"Shoot him, you fool!" the doc yelled at me.

"I shoot, we all go up in flames."

"Paul!" he screamed. "Paul, don't do this. I have a daughter!"

He smiled sadly at him. "Don't we all."

The lighter fell in slow motion, it seemed. I let the doc go because it was pointless anymore.

The fatal liquid had created a wall of fire between them and us and then started to run for us as it chased the gasoline. I saw the suit swing out the door, leaving us all to our deaths.

We ran. The doctor took off, leaving us all, but Marley and I both had the same idea.

We couldn't leave the kids by the observation room. We ran to the cove of doors, all of them open from the alarms just like the others had been, but the kids had been too scared to leave their rooms. They joined us in the hall with some coaxing. We hadn't made any mother-child reunions though because they all seemed like they didn't know each other. I shook my head. I had hoped, but that meant…their mothers were gone.

But that would have to wait until later.

"Come on!" I yelled to them and we took off down the hall. Every hall reached a dead end and as the fire spread into the rooms and ceiling, our oxygen started to become scarce. The last hallway we hadn't been down was our last hope. I led the way, the adrenaline kicking in, keeping me focused, my head injury forgotten.

There were no windows, no access to the roof from ceiling panels because it was concrete, no doors that led anywhere but circles of more rooms… We were trapped. They had known that was the only way out and we'd never leave. Their secrets would die with us all, along with their evidence and their files.

Everyone must have seen my defeated look, because they began to cry. The lights cut out next, leaving us in the dark all except the glow from the fire creeping closer from the main hallway. We all sat or knelt on the floor. Between the coughing, hugging, and crying in the dark, there was no noise but the roar of the fire.

I pulled Marley to me, my hands lovingly caressing her face, and kissed her over and over again as slowly as possible. If this was the way I was going to die, then I was going to go out letting her know I loved her. Though we hadn't said the words didn't mean that I wasn't absolutely in love with her. And I wasn't going to say them now just because we were dying, because that would cheat her. Even in death, I didn't want that for her. So I showed her instead.

"I'm so glad that you smashed into me with your car," I said and smiled at her. "I wouldn't change a thing about meeting you except that I didn't get more time with you."

She sucked in a ragged breath and let her tears fall as she smiled. "You hit me, buddy."

"OK," I conceded, though it was absolutely not true. "I'll let you have that one this time." I caressed her cheek with my fingers, knowing there wouldn't be a *next time*. "You took my soul and wiped all the dirt away, sweetheart. You cured me of all that ached."

She bit her lip so hard, I thought it would bleed. "I'm so glad I hit you that day, too. I'm so glad that I got to see the Jude that no one else sees."

I gulped as she ran her thumb across the scar on my neck. "You never told me how you got this."

I gripped her tighter as the girls beside me cried harder. "It was the only time Biloxi ever got his hands on me." She sat enraptured, even with everything going on. She needed me to keep her focused on this and I wanted to give her that. "Mom and I had just gotten to Mississippi. We were checking into this little studio apartment that comes furnished with things you need. I went out to the car to get our last bag of clothes and someone grabbed me from behind and tackled me, smashing my chin into the concrete step." She winced on my behalf. "Not three seconds later, mom came out and hit him in the side of the head with a cast-iron skillet. We packed up our crap, lickety split, and she took care of me herself with butterfly bandages. She couldn't take me to the hospital...so it left a big scar."

"She saved you once again."

"She was always saving me."

She cried harder. "I wish I could have gotten to meet her."

I smiled, feeling the prick of tears surfacing, knowing my next words were true. "She would have fallen in love with you, too."

She kissed me hard and held on, her lips wet with tears. I felt someone jerking on my sleeve and looked down at the little boy Marley had saved.

He pointed to one of the kid's rooms. "What is it, buddy?"

"They caught me once," he said and ran for the room. I followed with Marley in tow. He pulled the closet open and in the top of it was a wood panel. I looked at him in surprise.

"They caught me once when I climbed up. It's just a lot of buttons and wires up there."

Marley laughed and kissed his cheek. "You're a genius."

He wiped it off as I grabbed the chair from the corner and slammed it open, looking inside. There was some smoke up there, which meant the air ducts were probably close to the fire. The fire would be up there soon, too. It was all wood.

I hopped down and grabbed him, shoving him into the hole and helped Marley go next. Then I ran to get the others in the hall. They went as quickly as they could, but by the time they were all helped up the hole, the fire had reached the room.

I scrambled to get up, but realized we needed a light of some kind. I searched and found a small pen light on the desk. I groaned, but took it anyway. It was better than nothing. I pushed off the chair and used my arms to pull me up, but my strength was nil. I made it, barely, and rolled onto my back, my legs still hanging out the hole, my head aching. I took a deep breath and sat up. Tossing the panel back over the hole, I bent on my knees panting for a few seconds to catch my breath as I shined my light, looking for...something. I couldn't stop. I couldn't let Marley down again.

If that little boy hadn't told us about it, we would be dead right then.

I pushed between them to get to the front and find a way out. There was nothing up there but ductwork, insulation, panel and fuse boxes, and the air conditioning units. We crept through the space, ducking for bracing boards and wires. There were still no windows, but I knew there had to be a way for the air to escape through there. I searched the deck and ceiling for any creases or cracks that would mean a door or panel of some kind, but when a scream from the back of the group shot out, I knew it was too late.

The fire had reached our level.

The women scrambled our way, corralling the children, but there was nowhere to go. We had escaped the fire in the hall only to be handed hope that had nowhere to take us. The adrenaline left me in a rush and I knelt down, unable to stand any longer. I thought Marley was going to be angry and yell for me to get up, but she didn't.

She knelt beside me and put my head in her lap. She looked at the back of my head and cried softly when her hand came back with blood on it. She stroked my hair as she said, "You did everything you could. I know you're tired. Go to sleep, Jude. When you wake up, you'll see your mom. And I'll see mine."

I didn't answer. I didn't know what to say. I lay back and prayed for sleep. She whimpered and rubbed my forehead with her palm and I wrapped my arm around her middle, pressing my face to her stomach to offer her my own comfort.

Over the roar of the fire creeping toward us, I heard a siren. A police siren. If I could hear it, then there had to be a hole of some kind in the structure for the sound to come through like that.

I sat up and saw the edge of a grated duct or vent above our heads. It wasn't huge, but I knew a body could fit through there. I got up, my vision swimming, and crawled over to it. I stood. It was in the highest part of the ceiling and wall. It was welded to the metal frame and all painted with the industrial paint in the same color.

When I pushed on it, nothing happened.

I reared back, checking to make sure no one was directly behind me, pulled the gun from my shoulder, and started firing. The shots went everywhere because I was so disoriented, but the bullets ran out and it got the job done. The grating of the vent started to grow bigger holes to weaken the frame. I took the butt of the rifle and banged it over and over and over in the center, hoping for it to give way.

I was so angry that I wasn't strong enough right then to do what needed to be done. I yelled, screamed in anger, and with one final blow the grate showed pity on me, letting go and falling out the other side. I looked back to the group. They were yellow in the glow of the fire, dirty and coughing.

The grate didn't give us any light, but I figured it was night by then, so I beckoned Marley's boy to me and somehow managed to hoist him onto my shoulder. He looked out, gripping the edge. "What do you see?" I asked.

He stuck half of himself through the hole and the rest of him disappeared.

Marley screamed, but I saw a spotlight, or helicopter light maybe, sweep across the opening and a face appeared. His helmet wasn't on, but I knew he was a fireman. I didn't even think. I grabbed the closest pregnant woman to me and made a step for her with my linked fingers. He helped her out, but it was slow going trying not to hurt the babies, unborn and born ones.

Marley was next and I took her arm, but she snatched it away. "If you think I'm leaving you, you're crazy."

She coaxed the children to the wall so we could help hoist them up. They weren't so bad and Marley and I got them all out. The fireman asked how many more and I told him. He yelled something down to the other man and they switched places. Then he beckoned the next woman to him.

I tried to help her, but my body just wouldn't let me. Every time I used force, my head pounded and it felt like I was going to pass out. So I did the only thing I could think of. I got down on all fours and let them step on my back to hoist themselves up. Marley helped steady them as they were taken from the window.

I held on, I tried to think, and wondered if this was the way my mother had escaped. The fire got closer, taking with it all the insulation in a quick puff. The wires bent and curved, dancing in the heat. The women were almost clear now, but the fire was so close that my face burned from the heat off it.

Marley jerked my face up, her own face scared and red. "Jude!" she screamed. "Get up!"

"I have to help them," I muttered.

"They're all gone. You saved them all, baby. I've been trying to wake you up for minutes now." Her tears made me ache. "Please get up. Why aren't you talking to me?"

"I am," I answered, but even I couldn't hear it. "I am," I said louder and she gasped happily.

"Let's go, now. You're awake. Just get out the window and they'll help you down and it will all be all right."

It was at that moment that all my clarity slammed back into me. The window was too high. She was shorter than I was and there was no way she'd get herself up there for them to help her out. She was trying to get me to go first, but there was no way in hell I was leaving her behind.

I knew she was going to fight me so I had to do it quick. I knew I'd only have one shot at it. So I kissed her, knowing it would be the last time. I framed her face with my hands and let my thumb travel down her nose one more time. When I heard a huge chunk of the floor cave in behind us, I went for it.

I bent and put her butt on my shoulder, hoisted her right to the window and felt all my relief as she was taken from my hands. I heard her screams, her begging me not to, but I had to. I had to. I couldn't let her down again.

I fell to the floor, unable to hold myself up and her cries for them to get me out drifted away. I heard them tell her the place was going to come down…

I was glad when my ears started ringing, because her crying for me broke my heart. I felt the floor on my face and was shocked at how hot it was. The ceiling on my right sagged and groaned before caving and shaking me where I laid. My eyes tried to fight it, to stay until the last second, but my body had a different plan and took me away.

The last thing I remembered before darkness was the lick of flames on my calf and a moment's pain before it was all sucked away to nothingness.

SEVENTEEN

Mom baked actual cookies that day. I remember that it was weird because we always ate cheap veggies and stuff like that. Cookies never made the cut.

"What's the occasion?" I asked and hopped up on the counter with her.

"I'm just celebrating something." She looked at me and her smile was small but genuine as it always was. She was probably celebrating me finishing school for the year, I had thought. She homeschooled me since I was four and she was more excited than I was for the break. We didn't break for summer though, like other kids. We took a break in the fall. It was her favorite time. We'd go drive and she'd force me to look at all the leaves changing into a hundred different colors. I hated it then, thought it was stupid. But back then, gas was only a dollar a gallon and it was the cheapest activity we had.

Then she'd stop, and if we were in a state with mountains or peaks or valleys, we get out and look out at it. She'd get the small smile that she wore now and we'd sit and talk about her when she was a kid.

But now, I really wanted to know what that smile was for. "Really, Mom. Spill. What's going on?"

She took a deep breath and put her hands on my shoulders. "Today, ten years ago, was the day that I gave you your freedom." I gave her a curious look, not understanding. She leaned in and kissed my forehead. "And you're going to do great things with this life. I just know it."

"Ah, come on, Mom."

"You're going to laugh, run for fun and not because you have to, you're going to eat cookies for no reason at all, find a job you love, a girl who adores you, friends who deserve you, a house that you can stay in forever, and you're going to love, baby. You're going to love with all that you are, down into your soul."

She cried and once again, my ten-year-old self didn't get why it was all so important. She had been celebrating the day she escaped the facility, the day she set me free. But the me *now* understood and I'd never, ever wanted my mom to be there with me more than right then.

Thank you, mom, for loving me enough that you fought for me.

I felt a tear slide from my eye and a cool hand wipe it away. "Jude," someone whispered in my ear.

I recognized the voice immediately and knew this wasn't a dream or heaven. It was real and my girl had found a way to save me. I opened my eyes. The lights were already turned down to a soft glow and there she was.

"Hey, sweetheart," my raspy voice told her.

She burst into this half cry half laugh thing and laid her forehead on mine as she refused to release the death grip on my hand. "Jude Ezra Jackson," she whispered. "You came back."

"I'll always come to you. How quickly you forget." I touched her hair, weaving my fingers into it to anchor her there. "Wow, you're so soft."

She leaned back a little and grinned, her cheeks stained with tears. "You are so not hitting on me right now."

"But I am," I told her, my voice sounding more clear. "Kiss me, sweetheart. I missed you."

She leaned in and let her soft lips touch mine in several caresses before she gave me the full pressure I craved. She kissed me once and then spoke angrily against my lips. "So, my life is worth more than yours, huh? You can just make the choice for me that I'm going to live and you aren't?"

"I couldn't let you down," I told her. "And I couldn't watch you die. And I couldn't let someone so beautiful inside out be taken from the world if I could stop it." She sobbed against my mouth, but I held tight. "And I wouldn't let your mom's sacrifice for you be all for nothing."

"Yeah? What about your mom?"

I smiled and touched the scar on her lip. "My mom would have wanted me to sacrifice anything for the girl I was in love with."

I could see the dam bursting in her, so I gently tugged her closer, pulling her onto the bed with me on her side so I could feel her everywhere, the blanket the only barrier keeping me from her. She slammed her mouth on mine and that was all I needed; the thumbs up that she was OK.

One of my calves was all wrapped up in gauze and hissed with a sting when I wiggled around, but that didn't stop me from putting my good knee between hers and letting my hands take a tour. When my palm reached just under her behind, I was heartbroken she wasn't in her shorts. Her skin called to me and I answered.

I gave her all that a man could give her in a hospital bed with wires coming out of every limb. And she gave it to me right back.

Somewhere in the middle of all those tugs and moans and kisses, that was the most killer make-out session I'd ever had, she said, "I fell in love with you a little the first time you let your thumb drift down my nose in that bar." I demonstrated since I loved doing it so much. "And I fell in love with you a little bit every day since then." She smiled and put my hand over her heart. "It's so full, it hurts."

The nurse was mighty upset to find us a few seconds after that statement on the bed that way. I secretly thanked her, for she may have been the only thing keeping Marley's virtue intact on that hospital bed.

I knew the promise of what was to come was going to be incredible.

She sat back in the chair and let the nurse do her job, but flat refused to relinquish my hand. The nurse said that only family was allowed in during exams and after hours.

"She is my family," I said sternly and looked at Marley's blue eyes with nothing but love for her.

I knew hospitals were bad for someone on the run, but if Marley brought me here and was calm about it, then all must be right in the world again. I didn't freak out. I trusted her and just welcomed the *being alive* part.

Marley was in green scrubs. She said she had showered there and everything. Not just because she had nowhere to go, but because she wouldn't leave my side. They tried to make her leave several times, but she just ignored them and they eventually left, she said. I smiled at her, my fierce girl.

Later, Marley finally brought it all up and told me that the police had arrested every person that left up the stairs that day that they could find based on witness testimony and the fact that all those women and children were trapped by them. Oh, and arson as well.

The suit was one of them.

She said the news said that evidence would have helped and not all charges would stick without it, but at least the company was toast and the murderers in custody.

I sagged in relief. She told me that it was going to be a big stink, the media was involved, and no one in the company was safe, not even the New York office that claimed to know nothing.

The BioGene stock plummeted.

I'd been in the hospital for only two days when I woke up. After I hoisted her up to the fireman, she said she threatened to dis*member* him if he didn't help me. So when he called down to me and got no answer, he hoisted Marley back down into the window and she wrapped a harness around me. They pulled me out and then sent the harness down for Marley, too. Not seven minutes after the ladder was lowered and everyone was being cared for, the building collapsed.

I hated that we'd lost all that evidence. And the stuff about her mom and mine. I... Wait.

"Where's my clothes?"

"Uh..." She looked around. "Under here." She pulled the *Personal Belongings* bag from under the bed and set it on my stomach. I used the button to sit up and dug through the bag to my pants pocket.

I grinned as I pulled the USB memory stick out. "Looky, looky."

She gasped. "Is that..."

"Yep. I copied everything that looked important from the computer for a rainy day. And I think it's pouring."

She laughed and kissed me. I sighed, feeling lighter than ever. "I'm so...happy right now. I just wish we could have gotten to at least look through our moms' files and stuff. But it's all gone." I twisted my lips. "All burned up."

She bit into her lip. "Well, I have a bag of my own." She plopped a bag that matched mine on my lap and pulled out the folders that I'd given her to keep.

My mouth fell open.

"They were in the back of my pants waistband the whole time, safe and sound."

Wow…a piece of my mom was right there in front of me. A piece of her history and her life, even though it was those bastard's notes…it was *my mom*.

We spent the entire night going through it all. We laughed, we cried—yes, *we* cried—and we got a slice of the closure we so desperately wanted. No, we couldn't bring them back, but we could remember them the way they were meant.

It didn't say exactly why they'd gone into the program, but from what we could gather it was some kind of vitamin they offered them and free medical care for them while they were pregnant. But the catch was they had to stay at the facility and be monitored during the pregnancy. It didn't take them all that long to figure out something was screwy when they didn't let them leave the room and began drawing blood every day.

Every. Daggum. Day.

The notes told us what they asked them, what they talked about, how many days they cried versus how many days they were silent. It talked about how the vitamins made the male growing in patient C bigger and the patient experienced no morning sickness. The female growing inside patient F had a stronger heartbeat than the rest and she kicked more often, and also caused no morning sickness for the patient.

My mom was passionate in her anger where Marley's was more reserved and just didn't understand why they picked her. My mom demanded to be released and had to be strapped to her bed on several occasions because she kept attacking the doctors. Marley's mom got to a point where she flat refused to acknowledge them when they came into her room. They both rebelled in their own way.

The notes just stopped for them both after a while. No explanation as to why except one word—rogue. Their termination date was the last thing listed.

In my mom's file was a disc. There wasn't one in Marley's and I could tell she was disappointed. I wasn't so sure. We had no idea what was on it. It might be something that we didn't even want to see. We got one of the nurses to let us borrow her laptop to put it in and see what was on it. I expected files of tests they performed, since there was no label on the disc, but when we put it in, a video popped up. I pressed play and there she was. I couldn't stop my gasp as I watched my mom sit on her bed, her belly pregnant with me, and she always kept her hand atop it, as if to protect me.

It was weeks of footage, but only an hour a day. It was random. Sometimes there would be a doctor asking questions in the room, sometimes she would be alone and the hour would pass with her sleeping. Sometimes she mumbled or whispered. I fast-forwarded it when her lips weren't moving to when they were. I heard her tell a doctor that she was starting to have Braxton Hicks contractions. Marley explained that meant practice contractions. Her body was preparing to have me.

The doctor left. She covered her belly with both of her hands and started to cry. I covered my mouth with my palm and started to turn it off, unable to watch my mother suffer anymore, when she started to whisper again. I turned it up as far as it would go, and we heard my mother's whispered promises to me, her unborn son that she had already named Jude.

She had been talking to me all those times she'd been mumbling. She said them so softly, like these words were just for me and not for them if they had been listening.

"Jude, your momma loves you already. I'm so sorry that I brought you here. I didn't know that men could be so cruel. I should have known that when someone offers you something that sounds too good to be true at just the time you need it, then it is. Your father was a good man. We got married young and pregnant right after that, but I loved that man. He was in the Army and was killed in Desert Storm. His parents offered to help me, but they didn't have any more money than I did. I was applying for jobs when I got a visit from a man. He said he worked for a company, a medical facility, and they made drugs for pregnant women. The drugs were safe and they would offer me a place to stay, food, all the free medical care I needed, and promised that I would owe them nothing when it was all over. All I had to do was take their vitamins and let them monitor me. A drug trial." She sniffed, pulling her knees up as far as her belly would allow. I'd never seen my mom so vulnerable before. "I did it because I thought I was helping you. I had no insurance, no way to pay for all the medical bills that were about to pile up, so I said yes. I knew something was off pretty quickly when they wouldn't let me call your father's parents and let them know how I was doing. And when they did the first of many amniocentesis," she rubbed her belly harder, "which is a test where they stick a needle through my belly, I knew that something awful was going on. I'm so sorry I brought you here, baby boy. I'm so sorry."

The video cut out after a few minutes of silence and the next one started. She was sleeping. The next one started and my breath caught. She wasn't pregnant anymore. She paced the room angrily, stomping and hitting the door with her foot with each pass. Finally, the door opened and a woman held a baby in her arms. Mom took him from her and gripped him to her, cooing and crying that it was all right. The woman left and Mom laid me on the bed. She lifted my little shirt and gasped at seeing the IV port there in my skin. Even from that distance, my skin looked red and angry and I cried until she picked me back up.

Mom prowled the room for a few long minutes before she stopped. She slowly looked toward the closet, her back straightening with determination. She opened the closet and pretended to look for something, but her eyes never left the panel in the ceiling. Marley gripped my arm tighter as we realized the same thing.

"That's how she escaped," Marley said in awe. "We escaped the same way as your mom."

I didn't know how that was possible, or how she got down with me, but it happened somehow.

Mom spoke clearly, for all to hear, but only we would understand the true meaning of her words. "Even your death is better than your torture."

We watched her as she rocked and fed me for hours more on the video. Finally, she fell asleep, but she didn't let go of me. She held me, kissing my head over and over, as she sang the same song she always sang to me. "Hey, Jude…"

The video ended and there was no more after that. I knew why. She had escaped. *We* had escaped. She and I. I just stared at the screen until I felt Marley's hand on my cheek. She bit her lip and used her thumb to wipe under my eye. I wasn't embarrassed. The woman gave me everything, even her own life, the least I owed her was a few tears.

Marley took the laptop away and crawled into bed with me, wrapping her arms around me and letting me wallow in her warmth as I was finally able to mourn my mom. She ran her fingers through my hair with my head on her chest and we didn't say a word. We didn't need to.

Marley cries were soft and when they became harder, I knew her sadness had switched from my mom to hers. I sat up and wrapped her tightly in my arms that were never, ever letting her go. She spent all night by my side on the bed with me. Her tears eventually dried up, the guilt for the way she blamed and hated her mother was wiped away by the pages in that file.

The pregnant women, mothers, and a few of the children came to see me the next day. Even the city came and gave me a plaque saying how I'd expressed exceptional heroism in the face of danger and risked my life to save others. Marley cried some more, but it was all happiness this time. They took a couple of pictures and the mayor said he was honored to be pictured with a real-life hero.

I wasn't a hero; I was just a guy with an opportunity to be heroic. Marley's mom? And my mom? They were the real heroes. For they not only gave their lives for us, they sacrificed it willingly so that we could live.

So that we could fall in love.

So that fate could bring us to each other.

So that we could smash into each other.

So that we could live happily…ever after.

EIGHTEEN

"I don't see any abnormalities. I ran every test I could think of. You both have a higher white blood cell count, but that's not going to cause any problems. Other than that, you're both perfectly healthy."

"What does that mean, exactly?" I asked him.

"It means you probably don't get as sick as other people. Other than that..." I looked over at Marley. I'd never been sick a day in my life. Her face suggested the same for her.

I nodded and took Marley's hand as we left, slowly for my benefit. "Thanks, Doc. We appreciate it."

My leg was still not right. The skin and look of it would never be the same, they told me. It hurt to walk on, the jiggle of my muscle with each step sent shooting pain through it, but for the most part, I was pretty normal again.

When we stepped out of his office, Marley sighed loudly. "Oh, my gosh. Thank you, thank you," she said with her eyes closed.

"We can relax now." I squeezed her fingers as I opened her door. "Everything is all right and it's going to be fine."

She squealed happily and threw her arms around my neck before kissing my cheek and leaning back to hop in. I laughed as I went to the driver's side of the beautiful old Chevy truck we still possessed.

We went back to Alabama so Marley could finish her classes. And I could finish my Spanish credit. Yay...

The police were mighty happy to get the USB drive and the files we had. They said it was a miracle we had taken it. We copied everything of our moms' to keep and passed everything else over. They said it was a sure-fire open-closed case now, thanks to us. Honestly, I didn't even want to follow it and see what happened, I just knew things were going to work out, but we did have to go in just once for our testimony. Man, that sucked. Watching Marley get up there and try to hold it together sucked so badly. Once it was done, we walked away and never looked back.

They offered to put us into some kind of witness protection or something, but with Biloxi gone and everyone else in prison or jobless or...whatever, everyone decided we didn't need that. Besides, if we did that, Marley's credits for college would go away and I didn't have the heart to make her start over from scratch. So, we said no thanks and decided to start a new life. One where running wasn't a requirement.

I started working full-time. When we got back to town, I went and explained everything to Pepe. I told him that was why I wanted to be under the radar, why I asked him to pay me under the table, all of it. He met Marley and told me to watch out for beautiful woman. Then he blew my mind by offering me a general manager position since he fired his *ex*-wife and the position was available. I accepted and, not even a few weeks later, Pepe decided he wanted to branch out, open a few chain stores in the state, and gave me one to run since he trusted me.

A pretty nice little raise came with that and I couldn't believe it had happened. We were moving to Georgia and Marley was transferring her credits to UGA. She got some assistance with the tuition and we would come up with the rest. It was what she wanted and somehow, some way I was going to see it to fruition.

We had been staying in my crappy apartment for the past five weeks since we'd been back. And we started preparing to move into a bigger crappy apartment in Athens that wasn't in the college district and was on the quiet edge of town. The party scene, the college life…wasn't who I was anymore.

Boxes lined my wall, not many mind you since we didn't have much of anything, but what we had was ready to go. I couldn't wait to move.

My past was catching up to me in this town. I'd run into more than one girl who wanted to rehash or relive a time we'd spent together. On more than one occasion, Marley had been with me either walking around campus or out for groceries or dinner. The fact that they treated her as if she were invisible pissed me off royally.

Catty, petty girls.

So as Marley got her last day stuff settled at school, I was busy cleaning up and getting all the trash taken care of in the apartment.

When there was a knock on the door, I wasn't surprised. I knew exactly who it was. There was only one girl who I had been avoiding that hadn't managed to catch me yet. And only one girl that would show up at my house even knowing about Marley.

I pulled a shirt on real quick and opened the door. "Hey, Kate," I said evenly.

She bit her lip, chewing on it really. "Hey."

She heard about Marley. She wasn't herself. She wanted me to tell her it was just rumors. "I'm leaving. We're moving to Georgia. We leave tomorrow."

"We," she said wryly. "Jude Jackson has an official 'we' with someone?"

I paused to keep calm and then nodded. "Yeah."

"How come that couldn't have been me?" she asked and stepped noticeably closer. "Can I come in?"

I really didn't want to let her. She'd only ever been here twice before and we didn't spend the time here talking. Gah...I pressed my palms into my eyes. "No, Kate." I came out and shut the door, coaxing her to sit on the steps with me. "I'd rather sit out here."

"You're not even going to give me a chance to convince you that I'm better for you, are you?" She hadn't sat down yet.

I looked up at her. "No. I don't need convincing that I'm in love with the girl that lives here with me."

She sat with a huff. "I would've done anything for you."

I sighed. I had been such a bastard. But this girl was an idiot in her own right. "Kate, I know that. And that's your first mistake."

She parted her lips in surprise and huffed. "What?"

"I'm saying this…as your friend. I was an ass. I never called you unless I wanted something from you. Never took you on a date, or even just to get some food. Never asked you how classes were going. I treated you horribly-"

"The sex was great though, wasn't it?" she asked, forgetting everything I just said. Her eyes were hopeful.

"Yeah," I admitted, resigned. "The sex was great. But sex doesn't equal love, Kate." She visibly deflated. "I'm sorry. I'm so sorry for being such a jerk. You need to find someone who wants more than sex. If he doesn't call you and see how you're doing or see if you wanna catch a movie or take you to your favorite restaurant or just talk and laugh at stupid things, then he's not the guy for you."

She was angry, understandably, but didn't seem as broken up as before. I relaxed a little. "Do you do all those things for that girl?"

I nodded.

I was the best kind of whipped for that girl. She never even asked me to pick her up from school, I did it because I wanted to. She never had to wonder if I was going to kiss her or ask how school went and listen to her groan about her professors when she got into the car. She never had to wonder if we were going out on Sunday morning for breakfast like an old married couple at the cheap diner and then go sit at the lake and give our crumbs to the ducks as we people watched. Or if I was going to kiss her under the big willow tree I found for her there and not care who was watching.

"Why didn't you do all those things for me?" she asked, her eyes wide and wanting.

With my elbows on my knees and my hand in my hair, I said as softly as I could. "Because I wasn't in love with you, Kate." I sighed and sat up straight.

She was completely unaware of my mental checklist. I hated that she thought so little of herself that she would stoop to begging on my porch, and this wasn't the first time. She still stared at me. "I wasn't where I was supposed to be…in my mind, in my life. I was…angry and took out my anger on everyone else. On you."

"You never were angry with me. You never hurt me."

"But I did, Kate," I said in exasperation. "Look at you. I did hurt you." She licked her lips and sighed, knowing I was right. "I was an ass and I deserve for you to be angry with me. Don't let some guy do to you what I did. Don't let them use you. You're worth more than that."

Her face tightened, realization setting in. "You're in love with her, aren't you?"

"Yes," I said firmly.

"There's no going back?" Her final plea.

I shook my head and needed to make this perfectly clear for her. "Not a chance. She's it for me."

She stood, so I stood. She turned full-on to look at me. I saw Marley come around the corner of the bottom of the stairs just as Kate reached out and put her arms around my neck. Marley didn't look happy as she looked up the steps at me with another girl in my arms, but she didn't look surprised either.

Daggum.

How long had she been there? How much had she heard?

I pulled back, setting her away. I didn't want to touch her more than I had to. "Bye, Kate."

"Just one more thing," she stalled, looking down at Marley, with a sad expression. "What does she have that I don't?"

"It's not a laundry list. It's not something you pick and choose about someone. It either works or it doesn't." She didn't seem convinced as she swung her gaze back to mine. I decided to be truthful. "She didn't chase me." Her eyes grew wide at that. "A forever kind of girl not only looks for a guy that loves her for her, but accepts nothing less than respect. I hope you find what you're looking for."

She scoffed as she turned to go. "Doubtful."

Marley stayed where she was, only leaning against the wall to let her go by. Kate didn't say anything to Marley, but she was staring her down and didn't stop until she was past her. When Marley came up the stairs, after a long pause at the bottom, she didn't look up, only down at the stairs as she walked.

I waited for her there and when she finally reached the top, her books in her hand and her purse over her shoulder, she lifted her head. She looked reserved and smiled sadly. "Hey."

"Hey," I said low. "I'm sorry about that."

"It's understandable that you dated someone before me," she reasoned.

"I didn't date her."

She twisted her lips. "I heard."

Knew it. Daggumit.

"Marley-"

"It's all right, Jude." She sat down on the step and I followed suit. I wanted to touch her, but had never had a relationship before. I didn't know the drill. Was she going to force me to sleep on the couch or something for this?

She leaned down into my line of sight and gave me a weird look. "You look like I'm about to sentence you to the guillotine."

I ticked my head to the side. "Are you? I've never done this before. Never dated before. Never had someone to…" I laughed under my breath, "…answer to before. Even before girls, I was a kid when my mom died. I was on my own, always doing whatever the hell I wanted."

She tried to keep her face straight. "And you want to do whatever you want. That's what you're saying?"

"No." Screw rules, if there were any. I slid closer and touched her cheek. "No, I don't want that. I'm just saying that I don't know what my ex…or…whatever you want to call her, showing up at the house when you're not here means."

She showed the first signs of a smile. "It means life is messy."

"So…you don't want to hurt me?"

"Define hurt."

I chuckled, leaning closer. "You don't want to de-ball me?"

She laughed, putting her hand on my knee. Good sign. "No. I think your balls are safe where they are."

"I just…" I shook my head, knowing it was time for all this to come to a head, but not liking it.

But I totally deserved it, every bit of it, for being such a jerk. "I hate that you have to see even more of the person I was before you. He wasn't a nice guy." She knew that firsthand. "I hate that he's bringing his past with him."

"His past will be just that tomorrow when we leave for Athens." She swallowed. "You needed to see her before you left."

"Why? It didn't make me feel better about it. I still feel like a piece of crap that I hurt her."

"But she feels better."

I grimaced. "Maybe you didn't see the whole thing, then."

"I walked up right behind her. When I saw her knock, I waited. I figured whoever she was she needed to see you."

"What if I had brought her in the house?"

The first night Marley slept in the house with me, I refused to sleep on the bed. We slept on the pullout sofa that night and every night since because I just couldn't do it. I couldn't let Marley be tainted by who I used to be.

"I knew you wouldn't," she said with certainty.

"How?"

She brought her palm to my cheek. "You wouldn't even let me sleep on the bed, Jude. I can...imagine why."

I closed my eyes for a couple of seconds. "She doesn't feel better for coming here. She probably feels worse."

"She doesn't," she assured. "Seeing you happy will help her get over it. She's hurt now, but the next guy that she goes head-first in with will be a good guy for her."

"How do you know?"

"Because she loves you…in her own small way and you told her that she was worth something."

I didn't know what else to say. "I'm sorry."

The only thing we seemed to tiff about was sex. She wanted to, to replace a bad memory with a good one. I got that, but if that was the kind of pressure on this thing, then I wanted it to be more than just a good time. I wanted it to be magical for her. Magical enough to make every bad thing go away. And I wanted to be different with her than I had with the others. I wanted to wait and see what life could be like when I was the gentleman my mom had always wanted me to be.

"Don't be sorry." She reached back and touched the picture of her mom in her back pocket. She always had it with her now. "Everything that happened to us brought me you."

I shook my head and pulled her up to sit on my lap. "That was a good line."

"Wasn't it?" she laughed, remnants of her sad smile still hanging on. "I should be an author. That was so poetic."

"Thank you for understanding. For not being insecure about us. I can imagine any other girl would have had a fit to find that when she came home."

She smiled. "I am not any other girl."

I pulled her closer and put her arms around my neck. "I am so in love with you, sweetheart."

She smiled happily. "I love you, and that's why I'm not worried."

She accepted my kiss, and with her sideways on my lap, she took everything I gave her.

"Good for nothing kids!" I leaned back swiftly to see my neighbor. "Take your half-naked selves back into your apartment and quit with the public indecency."

"Mr. Fowler, I'm sorry. I was just apologizing-"

"Ack. Whatever. Just stop making whoopee on my front porch!"

Marley had stopped gasping at Mr. Fowler's meanness long ago. She just pressed her lips together.

"Mr. Fowler, this is not your front porch. The stairs are closer to my porch than yours, if you want to get technical."

"Young folks today got no respect." He paced and looked over the railing. "Your loud music and drugs and parties 'til one a.m. and pizza every night!"

"I'm only guilty of one of those and if you ever want a slice, come on over."

"Ack." That noise was his favorite sound. He leaned back up and then he smiled. I balked. He knew how to smile? He looked past us to a slightly younger woman coming by us on the stairs. "Marlena," he growled in a playful voice.

I threw up in my mouth.

"Billy Bob," she crooned. They locked lips in a way that was definitely more private than anything I'd done with Marley in public. I was about to upchuck and she was laughing into my shoulder. Marlena leaned back and batted her eyelashes. "Ready for a night on the town, big boy."

"Ready, buttercup."

We stood so they could leave, but he said he forgot something inside. So he opened the door for her, and when she went in, he winked at me. Winked! I stood silently and watched him shut the door. Marley turned to me once they were gone and laughed. "Mr. Fowler's got game!"

"I can't believe you just said that."

She laughed harder and wrapped her arms around my neck. "Wanna order pizza tonight?" She kissed me slowly.

"Uh huh," I said against her mouth.

"Wanna watch a movie?" She kissed me again.

"Uh huh," I said lower.

"Wanna finish what you started a few minutes ago?" She took my bottom lip between her teeth and tugged.

I hoisted her up, wrapping her legs around my middle. "Uh huh."

"Let's go then…big boy."

I laughed so hard, I pushed her to the wall to keep her from falling for a second before hoisting her up higher and walking to our apartment for the very last night. "Sure thing, buttercup."

EPILOGUE

To say I was sweating bullets would be a serious understatement. We had lived in Athens for three months now. She went to school full-time and I worked a real live nine-to-five job for the first time ever. Marley felt strange letting me be the one taking care of the bills, but if she worked after school, I'd never see her.

And I wanted to be the one taking care of her. No one ever had before, and I loved holding that title. And I loved *her.*

The lady at the shop had brought out a huge rack of rings, but none of them were *her.* So I left, decided to go browse around somewhere else for a while, and stopped at an antique place. I hoped they had some older baubles that I could look at, but when she started pulling the rings she kept locked up in the case out, I put my hand up to stop her.

It was the one and I didn't need to look any further. Now why hadn't it been that easy at the jewelry shop? Because Marley wasn't some materialistic girl. She wanted something that *meant something*. And this ring had meant something to someone at one time.

It was sterling silver and the diamond was square cut instead of round. I didn't know if that mattered for the ring I was going to ask her to marry me with or not, but I took it out and it fit on my pinky. I had this strange feeling that it would fit her just right as I looked at the sparkly square with two smaller square ones on each side.

I hadn't planned to buy a ring today, just get a feel for them and then get her size and all that stuff later on the sly, maybe plan some romantic dinner and ask her.

But this felt so right. I didn't want to wait, and seeing this ring just made me realize how perfect it all was. It should be based on a feeling, not a cheesy plan to get her to say yes in front of strangers and have them clap and 'aww'.

This was all in my gut and my gut said to ask that girl to marry me tonight. The lady was shocked when I told her I'd take it.

To be honest, we were doing all right finance wise, but by no means doing so amazing that I could afford some crazy expensive ring. I made enough to pay for her school books and for us to be comfortable. If we wanted to go grab a bite to eat, we could. If we wanted to go to the movies, we did. That's all that I ever wanted was to have a way to take care of her comfortably where we weren't struggling and she never felt like her home was in jeopardy. I still caught her eating with her fingers all the time, but it was cute, really. It was just one of those things that stuck with her and would always remind us that life sometimes hands you trials to get through. But when it's done, when it's all over, you're a better person for it, you appreciate your life that much more.

I found Marley because of it.

The woman asked to wrap up the ring for me, but I told her I'd just keep it on my finger. That I was going to ask her right that second and the ring was fine right where it was.

She stopped after putting the tray away and looked at me. "So where are you going to ask her? Do you have a big day planned?"

"I don't know. I don't have a plan. Whatever feels right, I guess."

I didn't know why I was telling her all that, but it was just spilling out. She handed me back my credit card—my very first credit card—and smiled. "Good luck, young man."

I smiled, but I didn't need luck. She was going to say yes. I wasn't nervous about that. I was just nervous that she would think it was too soon and too crazy after only five months. I got into the old Chevy truck and drove across town to pick her up from school. We still only had one vehicle, but I liked picking her up. I liked protecting her.

She was sitting on the bench with one of her professors when I pulled up. She was discussing something in depth with him and she just kept nodding, looking shocked.

I waited, but wanted to rush out there like a caveman. When she finally stood, she waved to him and climbed in. I put the truck in gear and let her collect her thoughts. Eventually, she put all her crap down and scooted over in the seat next to me.

I relaxed and lifted my arm around her on the back of the seat. "So…" she started, "my professor said that he wants me to be his TA next year."

I squinted. "I don't know much about it, but I thought you had to be a junior to be a teacher's assistant."

"Usually, that's the case, but he said since I scored…wait for it…the highest," she did jazz hands, "grade in the class, he said he'll make an exception and thinks I'll be great at it. Can you believe that?"

I laughed. "Of course I can."

"Really?" she said, animated. "Cause he sure shocked the pants off me."

I scowled at her, switching from her to the road. "Don't make professor and pants-off references in the same sentence."

"Ahh," she crooned and leaned up to kiss my cheek. "He's totally married with a baby on the way."

"You mean I'm so ruggedly handsome that you can't even see another guy. That's what you meant, right?"

She giggled. "Of course, baby."

I didn't go home. I kept driving until we came upon the same willow tree we always sat under at the park. She leaned up. "We don't have any crumbs for the ducks."

"They'll get over it." I grinned and pulled her from my side of the truck. I walked with her slowly with her hand in mine, her arm brushing mine. The park was getting darker as the sun went down, but there was still plenty of light. A yellow and orange sky had settled over us and with the lake there, it was like a freaking postcard.

We stood in the middle of the swaying branches and watched the ducks as they came up the shore, begging for what we didn't have.

"Aww. Poor guys," she said and laughed as they walked back and forth like they had just missed it.

"Do you love it here?"

She looked at me and smiled for my sudden, random question. "Yeah, I do."

"You want to stay here? Like, even after school?"

"Uh...yeah. I love the town. And your job is here and Pepe won't ever get rid of you."

"Do you want me to buy you a house here? Our own house that will be all ours and no one can take it away from us?"

I watched her chest rise and fall as she inhaled shakily. "Yes. I do want that."

"Do you...wanna get married right here, in this park, under our tree? The tree we found for your mom? The ducks can come, too."

She smiled, biting into her lip. "I like the sound of that."

"Do you want to marry me...right here, as soon as it can possibly happen?"

I waited for tears, but there were none. She just smiled. Oh, no. She thought I was joking? Then her smile rose and got wider, she bit her lip harder, her eyes finally took on the sheen of happiness I had been hoping for.

"You want me to be Mrs. Jackson?"

I nodded, leaning in and letting my nose rub hers as I did it. "I want you to be mine, officially, in front of God, and everyone, and the ducks."

She laughed, and then she sniffed a little, the first tear letting loose. She whispered hoarsely, saying, "Really?"

I was surprised by her reaction. "Didn't you think I'd want to marry you someday?"

"I hoped, but since you're so stuck on the no-sex rule-"

I cut in with a growly laugh. "I think we've done plenty of things to keep you satisfied, sweetheart."

She grinned and continued, "I figured you'd come up with a no-proposing-until-Marley's-twenty-seven rule, too."

I laughed, loving this girl so much. "No. No more rules," I said with emphasis.

She got my meaning and her lips parted. Her bottom lip began to quiver. "As soon as possible meaning…next month? Next week? Next weekend?" She grinned, the tears clinging to her lashes.

"Even that's not soon enough."

Then she laughed, cried some more, and jumped up in my arms. The park was empty and I was glad for it as I lifted her, pressing her spine gently to the tree. I took her wet kisses and licked at her mouth. She was barely controlling herself and it was making me wild. Her long skirt wasn't barrier enough for me and I felt so weak for her, but so strong with her.

The combination was heady and explosive.

My hand gripped her ribs as she pressed closer. I scooted my hand up past the side of her breast and then down, down. My palms loved on her behind while my lips loved on her mouth. My tongue loved on her tongue.

Soon, my body would love on her body.

I felt her hand in my back pocket, doing her own loving. I couldn't wait to feel her hands on me, to rob her of her breath with my hands claiming her skin. I let her lips go and smiled down at her, my grin so wide my cheeks hurt as the wind blew the branches around us. The whole setting was perfect, exactly what I wanted for when I asked her to marry me. I lifted my hand, showing her my pinky. "You going to say yes or not?"

She gasped and covered her mouth. I let her feet fall gently to the ground and took her left hand in mine. I looked at her expectedly and she nodded emphatically. I pulled it from my pinky, kissed her left ring finger, and slipped it on. It fit perfectly just like she fit with me.

"Jude," she complained in a happy sigh. "You didn't have to. I would have married you without it." She framed my face with her small, cool hands and grinned up at me. "Just like I don't want some insane wedding. I want a dress and a preacher and Pepe and you. And the ducks." I laughed. "And cake, obviously." I laughed harder. "That's all I need."

"And I love you for it."

"Did you plan this?" she asked.

I shook my head. "I went to look at rings and try to make a plan for one day. But I saw this ring and it all just seemed...right. I just...knew I didn't want to go another day without you knowing that I wanted you to be mine in all ways."

"And I love you for it."

"I love you more."

There was more people there than just Pepe. She had several professors and students come from school. I had a couple of employees and Pepe, with his new young wife. Our neighbors who lived in the apartment complex. My grandparents, my father's parents. Yep. I finally got up the courage to contact them and told them the big, crazy story. They were stunned to say the least. They thought Mom had just wanted nothing to do with them since they weren't her parents. Mom didn't have any family to contact. We looked.

And we realized that was one of the things that BioGene looked for in its test subjects. Someone that not too many people would look for.

Marley searched, too, but came up empty, so I hired a private detective to do some digging for her. Turned out that her mom left her dad for an unknown reason, but they weren't married. Marley found out who her father was and what he did for a living. His name was Dennis and he worked on oil rigs, gone months at the time. Unfortunately, he had passed away a few years back and had no relatives. We did find a half sister, Sarah, who was much older than Marley. They had begun to talk some on the phone, but she wasn't there at the wedding with us. It was a strange predicament. Marley's father had left Sarah's mother for Marley's mother, and then moved on to someone else after that, so...there was obviously some animosity from Sarah there, even though neither child had anything to do with that.

It was a work in progress, but it was nice to finally feel like we knew our mothers. My grandparents had visited twice since I'd found them, and yeah, things were awkward, but for the most part, they were just happy that I wanted them in my life.

In fact, they even paid for our honeymoon trip for us to Maui. I fought them hard on it, but in the end, they said they missed out on spoiling their grandson when I was a kid. They wanted to do it, so I let them. We were leaving tonight on our very first plane ride.

I couldn't wait for it. Any of it. Our lives weren't perfect, but we gripped what was left of it with all we had with a plan to fill it with new memories that would steal our breath.

But nothing else mattered as I watched her walk through her mom's willow tree to get to me. Her dress was long, simple, white, and beautiful. No one walked her down the aisle, but she was OK with that. When she got halfway there, *Hey, Jude* began to play. I felt my mouth open in surprise.

Marley's eyes held a secret and I knew right then that it was her. She was letting my mom be here with me on our day, in the only way she could be here. And Marley's mom was here in her own way as Marley pushed the willow branches aside and smiled, biting her lip.

As my mom sang to me in my memories, I welcomed a lifetime of new ones with the girl currently making her way to me. And when she reached me, I knew this was forever as my heart burst, full of sunshine and rays of happiness pushing out all the bad stuff.

The day she smashed into me wasn't just the best day of my life—it was the day that I became a man. I would spend an eternity making her happy, every hour of the day loving every inch of her, every minute remembering that she saved me.

When the preacher asked me if I would love and cherish this woman forever, I would tell him that I was way ahead of him.

Marley Jackson was mine, and I was hers, all smashed together for our happily ever after.

THE VERY END

PLAYLIST

Demons : Imagine Dragons
All I Want : Kodaline
Dust and Bones : Night Terrors of 1927
Let Them Feel Your Heartbeat : Silent Film
In My Veins : Andrew Belle
Give Me Love : Ed Sheeran
Biffy Clyro : Opposite
I Love You : Alex Clare
If So : Atlas Genius
Beneath Your Beautiful : Labrinth
Running Up That Hill : Placebo
The Shadow Proves the Sunshine : Switchfoot
Saved : Spill Canvas
Girls Like You : The Naked and Famous
Kiss Quick : Matt Nathanson
Back Seat : Atlas Genius
You Are : Colton Dixon
Whistle For the Choir : The Fratellis
Stubborn Love : The Lumineers
Hey, Jude : The Beatles

THANK YOU

Thank you to my girls, the HELLCATS, Michelle Leighton, Lila Felix, Amy Bartol, Samantha Young, Georgia Cates, Rachel Higginson, Angeline Kace, and Quinn Loftis. You girls are amazing at keeping me sane and I love you to pieces.

Jamie Magee, you are my new soul mate! (See what I did there?)

My street team, Sweet Street. I heart you so much for all your help and the way you rally together. You're awesome! Mwah!

Mary Smith - BooksAcrossAmerica, Mandy - IReadIndie, Candace Selph, Fabulous and Fun - Mike and Jenny, Little Bit of R&R - Ren, Kelly and Nazarea - Inkslinger PR, TSK TSK What To Read, Cynthia Shepp - Editing, Sarah - Okay Creations. You all are the best and helped immensely with this book and the ones before it. Thank you!

To my awesome readers, thank you for sticking with me. Fourteen books later, I've tried to keep things the same vibe while making each book different and fresh. Thanks for coming along for the ride.

About the Author

Shelly is a *New York Times* & *USA Today* Bestselling author from a small town in Georgia and loves everything about the south. She is wife to a fantastical husband and stay at home mom to two boisterous and mischievous boys who keep her on her toes. They currently reside in everywhere USA as they happily travel all over with her husband's job. She loves to spend time with her family, binge on candy corn, go out to eat at new restaurants, buy paperbacks at little bookstores, site see in the new areas they travel to, listen to music everywhere and also LOVES to read.

Her own books happen by accident and she revels in the writing and imagination process. She doesn't go anywhere without her notepad for fear of an idea creeping up and not being able to write it down immediately, even in the middle of the night, where her best ideas are born.

Shelly's website:

www.shellycrane.blogspot.com

Other series by Shelly Crane

Significance Series
Collide Series
Devour Series
Wide Awake
Smash Into You

Turn the page
for a peek of Shelly Crane's other series

Wide Awake

Useless Fact Number One

*A duck's quack doesn't echo
and no one knows why.*

Someone was speaking. No, he was *yelling*. It sounded angry, but my body refused to cooperate with my commands to open my eyes and be nosy. I tried to move my arms and again, there was no help from my limbs. It didn't strike me as odd until then.

I heard, "All I'm saying is that you need to be on time from now on." Then a slammed door startled me. I felt my lungs suck in breath that burned and hissed unlike anything I'd ever felt before. It was as if my lungs no longer performed that function and were protesting.

I heard a noise, a gaspy sound, and my cheek was touched by warm fingers. "Emma?" I tried to pry my eyes open and felt the glue that seemed to hold them hostage begin to let go. "Emma?"

Who was Emma? I felt the first sliver of light and tried to lift my arm to shield myself, but it wouldn't budge. Whoever was in the room with me must've seen me squint, because the light was doused almost immediately to a soft glow. My eyelids fluttered without strength. I tried to focus on the boy before me. Or maybe he was a man. He was somewhere in between. I didn't know who he was, but he seemed shocked that I was looking up at him.

"Emma, just hold on. I'm your physical therapist and you're in the hospital. Your..." he looked back toward the door, "parents aren't here right now, but we'll call them. Don't worry."

I looked quizzically at him. What was he was going on and on about? That was when I saw the tubes on my chest connecting my face to the monitors. The beeping felt like a knife through my brain. I looked at the stranger's hazel eyes and pleaded with him to explain.

He licked his lips and said softly, "Emma, you were in an accident. You've been in a coma. They weren't sure if...you'd wake up or not."

Of everything he just said, the only thing I could think was, 'Who's Emma?'

He leaned down to be more in my line of sight. "I'll be right back. I promise." Then he pressed a button on the side of the bed several times and went to the door. He was yelling again. I tried to shift my head to see him, but nothing of my body felt like mine. I started to panic, my breaths dragging from my lungs.

He came back to me and placed a hand on my arm. "Emma, stay calm, OK?"

I tried, I really did, but my body was freaking out without my permission. His face was suddenly surrounded by so many other faces. He was pushed aside and I felt my panic become uncontrollable.

I thrashed as much as I could, but felt the sting in my arm as they all chattered around me. They wouldn't even look me in the eye. That man...boy...was the only one who had even acknowledged me at all. The rest of them just scooted around each other like I wasn't important or wouldn't understand their purpose, like it was a job. Then I realized where I was and guessed it *was* their job.

My eyelids began to fight with me again and I cursed whoever it was that had stuck the needle into my arm. But as the confusion faded and the air become fuzzy, I welcomed the drugs that slid through my veins. It made the faces go away. It made my eyes close and I dreamed of things I knew nothing about.

My eyes felt lighter this time when they opened themselves. The fluttering felt more natural and I felt more alive. I could turn my head this time, too, and when I did I saw something disturbing.

There were strangers crying at my bedside.

The woman caught me looking her way and yelled, "Thank the Lord!" in a massive flourish that had me recoiling. She threw herself dramatically across the side of my bed and sobbed. I shifted my gaze awkwardly to the man and waited as he stood slowly, never taking his eyes from mine. "Emmie?" When I squinted he said, "Emma?"

When I went to speak this time, the tubes had been removed. I let my tongue snake out to taste my lips. They were dry. I was thirsty on a whole new level and glanced at the coffee cup stuck between his palms. He looked at it, too, and guessed what I wanted. He sprung to set the cup down quickly and fill an impossibly smaller cup with water from a plastic pitcher. I tried to take it from his fingers, but he must have sensed I needed help, because he held my hands with his and I gulped it down in one swig with his help. My arms ached at the small workout they were getting and again I wondered what I was doing there.

I made him fill it three more times before I was satisfied and then leaned back to the bed. I decided to try to get some answers. I started slow and careful. "Where am I?" I said. It felt like my voice was strong, but the noise that came out was raspy and grated.

"You're in the...hospital, Emmie," the woman sobbing on my bed explained. She smiled at me, her running mascara marring her pretty, painted face. "We thought we'd never get you back."

That stopped everything for me.

"What do you mean?" I whispered.

She frowned and glanced back at the man. He frowned, too. "What do you remember about your accident, sweetheart?"

I shook my head. "I don't remember anything." I thought hard. Actually, that statement was truer than I had intended it to be. I couldn't remember...anything. I sucked in a breath. "Who are you? Do you know something about my...accident?"

The woman's devastated face told me she knew everything, but there was apparently something I was missing. She threw her face back onto my bed and sobbed so loudly that the nurse came in. She looked at the man there. He glanced to me, a little hint of some betrayal that I couldn't understand in his eyes, before looking back to the nurse. "She must have amnesia."

The nurse ignored him and took my wrist in her hand to check my pulse. I wanted to glare at her. What the heck did my pulse have to do with anything at that moment? "Vitals are stable. How do you feel?" she asked me.

How did I feel? Was she for real? I rasped out my words. "I feel like there's something everyone isn't telling me."

She smiled sympathetically, a side of wryness there. "I'll get the doctor."

I looked up at her. She was short and petite, her blond hair in a bun and her dog and cat scrubs were crisp. I watched her go before looking to the man again.

"I don't understand what's going on. Did I…" A horrifying thought crossed my brain. The gasp I sucked in hurt my throat. "Did I kill someone? Did I hit them with my car or something? Is that why you're all being so weird?"

The man's own eyes began to fill then. I felt bad about that. I knew it was my fault, I just didn't know why. He rubbed the woman's back soothingly. He shook his head to dispel my theory and took a deep breath. A breath loaded with meaning and purpose. "Emmie…you were in an accident," he repeated once again that I was 'in an accident'. OK, I got that. I wanted him to move on to the part that explained the sobbing woman on my bed. He continued after a pause, "You were…walking home from a party after the football game. Someone…hit you. A hit and run, they said.

The person was never found. They left you there and eventually someone else came along and helped you. But you'd already lost a lot of blood and…" He shook his head vigorously. "Anyway, you've been here for six months. You were in a coma, Emmie."

I took in a lungful of air and uttered the question that I somehow knew was going to change my world. "Why do you keep calling me Emmie?"

He grimaced. "That's your name. Emma Walker. We always…called you Emmie."

"My name… Emma," I tasted the name. "I don't feel like an Emma."

He smiled sadly. "Oh, baby. I'm so sorry this happened to you."

The woman raised her head. "Emmie." She tried to smile through her tears. "Try to remember," she urged. "Remember what your favorite color is?" She nodded and answered for me, "Pastel Pink. That's what you were thinking, right?"

Pastel pink was the last color I would have ever picked. She tried again. "Or purple?"

Uh… "Are you sure I'm Emma?" She started to sob again and I felt bad, I did, but I needed answers. "Who are you?"

"We're your parents," the man answered. "I'm…Rhett. And your mother is Isabella. Issie…" he drawled distractedly.

"Rhett?" I asked. "Like in *Gone With the Wind*?"

He smiled. "That was your favorite movie when you were little."

I closed my mouth and felt the weight bear into my chest. I wasn't me. I had no idea who I was. These people claimed to know me and be my parents, but how could I just forget them? How could I forget a whole life?

I tried really hard to remember my *real* name, my *real* life, but nothing came. So, I threw my Hail Mary, my last attempt to prove that I wasn't crazy and didn't belong to these strangers, however nice they may be. "Do you have some pictures? Of me?"

In no time, two accordion albums were in my lap - one from the man's wallet and one from the woman's. I picked up the first, trying to sit up a bit. The man pressed the button to make the bed lean up and I waited awkwardly until it reached the upright position. I glanced at the first photo.

It was the man, the woman, two girls, and a boy. They were all standing in the sunlight in front of the Disneyland sign. The man was wearing a cheesy Mickey Mouse ears hat. I glanced at him and he smiled with hope. I hated to burst the little bubble that had formed for him, but I didn't recognize any of these people. The pictures proved nothing. "I don't know any of those people."

The woman seemed even more stunned, if possible. She stood finally and turned to go to the bathroom. She returned with a handheld mirror. She held the picture up in one hand and the mirror in the other, and I indulged her by looking. I have no idea why I was so dense to not understand what they had been implying, and what I had so blatantly missed.

I was *in* the photo.

I looked at the mirror and recognized the middle girl as the girl in the mirror. I took it from her hands and looked at myself. I turned my head side to side and squinted and grimaced. The girl was moving like I was, but I had no idea who she was. She looked as confused as I felt. I looked back at the picture and examined...myself. She was wearing a pink tank top with jean shorts. Her hair was in a perfect blonde ponytail and she had one hand on her hip and the other around the girl's shoulder. One of her legs was lifted a bit to lean on the toe. *Cheerleader* immediately rambled through my head. I almost vomited right there. "I'm a cheerleader?"

"Why, yes," she answered gently. "You love it."

My grimace spread. "I can't imagine myself loving that. Or pink."

It hit me then. Like really sank in. I had no idea who I was. I had forgotten a whole life that no longer belonged to me. I felt the tear slide down my cheek before the sob erupted from my throat. I pushed the pictures away, but kept the mirror. I turned to my side and buried my face in my pillow, clutching the mirror to my chest. My body did this little hiccup thing and I cried even harder because I couldn't even remember doing that before.

The man and woman continued to stand at the foot of my bed when the doctor came in. I looked at him through my wet lashes. When he spoke, his voice sounded familiar. "Emma, I'm sorry to have to tell you this, but it appears that you've developed amnesia from your accident. We'll have to run a lot of tests, but the good news is that in more cases than not, the amnesia is temporary."

I jolted and wiped my chin clear of tears. "You mean I could remember one day?"

"That's right."

"Don't get her hopes up," I heard from the doorway and turned to find the man-boy. My heart leapt a little. He was the only person that I remembered. Well, from when I woke up at least. He felt like some awkward lifeline I needed to latch onto. He shook his head. "Every case is different. She may never remember anything."

"Mason," the man yelled, making me jump at the volume of it, and shot daggers at him across my bed, "this doesn't concern you."

"She's been in my care for six months," he growled vehemently and then glanced at me. He did a double take when he saw that I was awake and looking at him. I had no idea what the expression on my face may have been, but he softened immediately and came to stand beside...my parents.

"Isabella. Rhett," he said and nodded to them as they did in turn. He was on a first name basis with my parents. He wasn't wearing scrubs like the nurse. He was in khakis and a button-up shirt, the sleeves rolled almost to his elbows. His name tag said "Mason Wright - Physical Therapy Asst.". He looked at me with affection that showed the truth behind his words. "I'm Mason, Emma. I've been doing all of your physical therapy while you've been...asleep."

"You look a little young," my mouth blurted. I covered my lips with my fingers, but he laughed like he was embarrassed.

He swiped his hand through his hair and glanced around the room. "Yeah... So anyway, I'll be continuing your care now that you're awake.

You'll have some muscle atrophy and some motor skills that will need to be honed again." I nodded. "But, from what I've seen from working with you these past months, I think you'll be fine in that department."

"Working with me? Like moving my legs while I was asleep?"

"Mmhmm. And your arms, too. It keeps your muscles from completely forgetting what they're supposed to do." He smiled.

I wanted to smile back at him, but feared that I didn't know how with this face. Plus, my body was exhausted just from this little interaction. He must have seen that, too, because he turned to the tall man who had yelled at him before. "She needs her rest."

"I know that," he said indignantly. "However, the news crew will be here later on." He turned a bright smile on the woman that was supposed to be my mother. "She'll do an interview with them and tell everyone all about her ordeal. I'm sure you could even get a deal on a big story to the-"

My father spoke up, putting a protective hand on my foot. "You set up an interview with the press the day she wakes up...and didn't even get our permission first?"

They all kept talking around me. Mason started defending me along with my parents. The man apologized half heartedly and I assumed he was the head doctor or some hospital administrator from the way he was acting.

My mind buzzed and cleared in intervals. I lost all track of time and eventually just turned to let my cheek press against the grainy pillow. My throat hurt from the tubes that had been keeping me alive.

Only to wake up to a reality that was more fiction than non.

My eyes still knew how to cry though and I tried to keep myself quiet as I let the tears fall. I thought I'd definitely earned them. Eventually the room quieted and the lights were turned off, all but the small lamp beside my bed. The phone on my bedside stand had a small list of numbers, for emergencies I assumed, but the name on the top of the card was what caught my eye. 'Regal City Hospice'.

Mason had been right. I wasn't even in a real hospital. They hadn't expected for me to wake up.

I wondered if that fact had put a kink in someone's plans.

End Of Preview

Available now in all formats.

Made in the USA
Lexington, KY
01 February 2014